James Payn

Gwendoline's Harvest

A Novel - Vol. 1

James Payn

Gwendoline's Harvest
A Novel - Vol. 1

ISBN/EAN: 9783337348151

Printed in Europe, USA, Canada, Australia, Japan

Cover: Foto ©Andreas Hilbeck / pixelio.de

More available books at **www.hansebooks.com**

GWENDOLINE'S HARVEST.

A Novel.

BY THE AUTHOR OF

'LOST SIR MASSINGBERD,' 'A PERFECT
TREASURE,' 'FOUND DEAD,' &c. &c.

IN TWO VOLUMES.

VOL. I.

LONDON:

TINSLEY BROTHERS, 18 CATHERINE ST., STRAND.

1870.

JOHN CHILDS AND SON, PRINTERS.

THIS BOOK

IS DEDICATED

TO

WILKIE COLLINS. ESQ.,

BY HIS FRIEND,

THE AUTHOR.

CONTENTS OF VOL. I.

THE SOWING.

CONTENTS.

THE RIPENING.

THE SOWING.

CHAPTER I.

ON THE RIVER TERRACE.

ON the left bank of a certain river in West Cornwall stood, a quarter of a century ago, an ancient residence, entitled for the most part by admiring tourists Belvidere Court, but more properly designated Bedivere. It was very old, and, for all that is known to the contrary, may have existed in some shape or other in King Arthur's day, and been the country-seat of Sir Bedivere himself, 'the last of all his knights;' though his stronghold it could

scarcely have been, by reason of its position. A wide bend of the river, which
was navigable for small boats to the sea,
afforded on its southern shore the space
upon which the edifice was built; and it
was commanded of course by the opposite
bank, as well as by that which—now a wall
of autumn foliage—towered steeply up behind it. The mansion, which was built of
stone, four-square, and with a courtyard
within, although an imposing and stately
edifice, exhibited traces not only of decay,
but of neglect. Time, that at last must
needs eat into the heart of stone itself, can
be bought off for a space like any other
barbarian; but small attempt had been
here made to come to terms with him.
The grass in the courtyard was growing
up among the cracked stones; the vast oak
staircases needed the carpenter as well as
the polisher; the wood-work of the huge
windows was rotten and worm-eaten, and
even the panes in some of the disused rooms

were missing—that is, having been broken, they had been removed altogether, to avoid the unsightliness they would otherwise have afforded.

From the river, however, Bedivere Court looked every inch a palace, and you would never have guessed that it was the home of poverty. The furniture of the reception-rooms was massive and striking, if its splendour was somewhat faded; and the thick pile of its immense carpets had in places grown thin and bare. The three drawing-rooms, *en suite*, had gilt and or-molu enough to furnish forth an acre of first floor in Mayfair or Belgravia; but in the daylight they showed dull and lustre-less, and the wax candles which would have been necessary to light them up would have consumed a week's income of their present proprietor. Sir Guy Treherne had been accustomed all his life to burn his candles at both ends, and the same fashion had held with his ancestors before him. In

Sir Guy's own sitting-room—a very snug
one, and in which no article of modern
luxury was wanting—hung a picture of
his great-grandfather, Sir Ralph, illustrat-
ive enough of this family peculiarity. It
represented a man of middle age, attired
in old velvet and tarnished lace, playing
at cards by himself with a mug of ale
before him. The legend ran that this noble
gentleman had gambled so freely, and with
such continuous ill-luck, that he could at
last find no man so poor as to contend
with him, and was driven to play Put, his
right hand against the left, for pots of beer.
The game had this advantage, that which-
ever won, Sir Ralph always emptied the
mug; but it was a sad falling-off from the
days when he could stake mine and moor
upon one turn of a card or one throw of
the dice; and eventually, tired of this
solitary sport, he had been compelled to
marry an heiress.

On the floor above, the best furnished

sleeping-room—and, indeed, it had nothing
to be desired which the London upholsterer
could supply—was again Sir Guy's; and
if you had only looked at those two cham-
bers, you would have said that the interior
of Bedivere Court was in all respects in
keeping with the stately character of its
external appearance—as seen, that is, from
the point of view we have already indicated. The rare 'excursion'-parties—
which, in those pre-railway days, came in
pleasure-boats up the river—would tarry
opposite the ' Court,' and express their innocent wishes that they were only half as
rich as the possessor of that imposing
structure; but if their desire could have
been gratified, it would probably have
proved even more disappointing than fulfilled desires usually are. It was only
strangers from a distance who could have
been under such a misapprehension at all.
Not a boatman at St Medards-on-Sea,
which was the nearest town; not a cottager

on the wide moorland that stretched to
southward, almost to the Land's End itself;
not an under-ground worker in those
western mines that had long passed from
the lavish hands of the Trehernes; but
knew that Sir Guy was almost as poor as
themselves, notwithstanding he still lived
at Bedivere Court, and that his daughter,
Miss Gwendoline, was the acknowledged
beauty of the county. And not only, it
might have been added, of the county, but
even of the London season. That very summer, Gwendoline Treherne had made a *suc-
cès* which had filled many a Belgravian ma-
tron with jealous bitterness. She had come,
had been seen, and conquered, at seventeen,
the previous year; and they had hoped she
would have gained her end, and left the field
free for others perhaps not less favoured by
nature than herself, although they might
have lacked that imperial grace of which
they did not deny her the possession.
Fashion, more honest (because more auda-

cious) than mere Gentility, allows some
merits even in a rival, and it was confessed
on all hands that a more magnificent creature had never courtesied at St James's than
Gwendoline Treherne. Those were not
the days of chignons, and the genuineness
of those masses of bright brown hair, that
fell on either side of her broad white brow,
and would have rippled to her heels but
for the pearls that held them, was never
called in question. Her complexion, although exquisitely fair, was almost colour-
less; and it was urged that those splendid
eyes gazed, from under their long black
lashes, with too little interest upon the
whirl and glitter of the world, for one so
new to it; that those fine features, faultless
as they were in form, somewhat lacked expression. None could doubt that she had
wit, but that again, it was said, was of too
mature a sort; too mocking and too worldly even for the idle jesting throng amid
whom her lot was cast. She sang, she

played, and in none of those accomplishments which Fashion has imposed on those
who aspire to be her favourites, acquitted
herself otherwise than well; but in these
she failed to captivate, because it was plain
to all that she herself took no pleasure in
them. It was also hinted, by persons of
judgment of her own sex, that in a few
years Gwendoline Treherne would grow
'horribly coarse'—contract too much of
what is scientifically termed adipose de-
posit; and indeed, in this Hebe of eighteen, there was something—though it was
as much owing to her mature manner as to
her rounded charms—that reminded one
also of Juno. The fact was, her form was
one of those which Nature only now and
then permits herself to build, lest it should
discredit the rest of her human handiwork.
Graceful in youth—graceful in womanhood
—graceful, or possessing something closely
akin to grace, in age itself; strong, yet
supple; delicate, yet enduring; and which,

having suffered, shows no trace of Sorrow's plough-share even until the end. Even at eighteen, Gwendoline had had experiences which would have marred the beauty of some girls for life, but there was not a line on that white brow to tell of them, nor one reflex of regret even in the most secret depths of those grand eyes.

Mark her now as she stands alone in the late but sultry autumn evening, with one hand on the balustrade of the terrace, and her queenly head turned slightly to one side, to catch an expected sound—the beat of oars upon the river. So motionless, she might have been a statue, save for the quick rise and fall of the fair bosom, which seems to resent the restraint even of its scant muslin prison. She is attired, though the materials of her dress are simple enough, in the height (or rather lowness) of the prevailing fashion; her noble head has no covering save that which bountiful Nature has bestowed upon it, and her round white

arms are bare. If she had had a mother, or
indeed any prudent person whatever to look
after her, she would surely at that late hour
have worn at least a shawl; but she is a
stranger, and has ever been so, to the
veriest common-places of affection and
domestic care; nor is there one of that
scanty household, including simple Fanny,
her own maid, who dares interfere even in
her own behalf with Miss Gwendoline's
caprices.

The expected oar-stroke is heard at
last, dull in the distance, and silver-sharp
as it draws nigh, and a light skiff shoots
up to the terrace stairs. At the first sound,
she withdraws into the square stone cham-
ber—which, half arbour, half greenhouse,
stands at the extremity of the river-front-
age—and there awaits the oarsman; it is
not the first time that he has found her
there, for it is her accepted lover, Piers
Mostyn.

'You are late to-night, dear Piers,'

says she, in a tone that certainly lacks no tenderness of expression; 'and yet I told you papa would be away by six o'clock'—

'And not return until to-morrow,' added he, embracing her; 'that will give us the whole morning together, Gwendoline.'

That this handsome young fellow with the short curly hair and blonde moustache, that contrast so strongly with cheeks bronzed by the southern sun, was in love with her, was evident enough, and yet he called her by no pet name, such as love delights in. She was Gwendoline to him, as to her father and to all the world.

'No, Piers; you will not see me to-morrow, nor at all again for many a long day,' returned she calmly; 'so you must make the most of me while you can.'

He kissed her fondly, as he well might do on such an invitation, and running his fingers through her ample tresses, sighed, somewhat wearily: 'What new enigma is

this, my darling? You have always something in that scheming brain of yours to
trouble me with. I sometimes wish that
you were a little more like other girls.'

'Like your cousin Maude may be, for
instance?' answered she quickly, and over
her pale face there came a sudden glow of
scarlet.

'Now, don't be foolish, dear. How can
you be so jealous of a shadow?—for she *is*
but a shadow compared with you, my empress! I only meant that when I would
have you all love and tenderness, you so
often chill me with the recollection of our
penniless condition, and the obstacles that
intervene between us and happiness.'

'It is better so, Piers: we must look
difficulties in the face if we would overcome them.'

'Well, I look at them, but they get no
smaller for that,' answered the young man,
with a touch of petulance. 'It is only
when I look at you that I forget them.'

'My darling Piers!'

To one who saw her, heard her now, it would have seemed ridiculous enough that any one should have ever said that Gwendoline's voice was wanting in flexibility, her features in expression, her eyes in passionate tenderness. For a brief space she seemed as ready as her lover himself to forget, in their mutual caresses, the gulf, so difficult to be bridged by marriage, between the penniless daughter of Sir Guy and the worse than penniless Piers Mostyn, the younger brother of a childless but still youthful lord, and whose slender patrimony was already exceeded by his debts. She was, however, the first to recall this stubborn fact to her remembrance—and to his.

'Dear Piers,' said she, 'if you really love me as you profess to do, you must listen seriously to what I have to say, and abide by it. I have had a long talk with papa to-day. He has placed my future position before me quite unreservedly.'

'I can easily believe it, Gwendoline,' returned the other with a bitter smile; 'Sir Guy can be a very plain speaker when he chooses. I have had experience of that myself.'

'Nevertheless, since he has only stated what is the fact, it is worth our best attention, Piers;' and she touched his somewhat effeminate cheek with her white hand, and pushed him gently from her. 'You must learn to live away from me, my own.'

'Let me have these to comfort me,' said he, snatching her fingers, and covering them with kisses; 'then, when you come to speak of parting, it will seem less bitter.'

CHAPTER II.

PLAIN SPEAKING.

'You have said papa can speak plainly, Piers, and you are right; moreover, he never loses his temper. He called me into his room to-day, and referred to my having met you here the other evening — who could have told him, I cannot guess, but he has found it out—as coolly as though you had been your brother, Lord Luttrel.'

'Who, had he been a bachelor, would scarcely have suited Sir Guy better,' observed Piers parenthetically. 'The estate is dipped deeper than I had thought, and

if he were to die childless to-morrow, I
should still be but a poor man.'

'Then, even *that* chance may be put
out of the question,' observed Gwendoline
significantly; 'and there is all the more
reason for your laying to heart what I
have now to say. You called me just now
your empress: Piers, I am obliged to you
for the compliment, but, as you don't happen to be King Cophetua, I am not likely,
so far as you are concerned, to be other
than I am—"a beggar-maid." Yes, Piers;
not merely a girl with an inadequate por-
tion, you must understand, but an absolutely penniless one. Even that tumble-
down old house yonder is only my home
so long as papa lives, nor has he one single
shilling to leave behind him.'

'Nay, Gwendoline; I know that you
will be poor enough, but your father has
surely exaggerated the case; it is impossible'—

'Nothing is impossible, Piers,' interrupted she gravely, 'when a man has sunk the remnant of his fortune in a life-annuity.'

'What! with a daughter absolutely dependent upon him? Do you mean to tell me that Sir Guy'—

'Nay, do not let us discuss the selfishness of man, Piers, because it is an extensive subject, and the night is late,' observed Gwendoline with cynical calm. 'Let us rather take matters as they are, and make the best of them. Papa's notion is—if his morality has any interest for you —that he has invested a considerable sum in my education, in my wardrobe, and in my *début* in London last year, and that I must live upon what profit I can get out of them, and look for nothing more from him. He is so good as to say that I have very considerable attractions of my own, which, in combination with what he has done for me, ought, it seems, to make my future position quite secure. He informs me too that men will bid higher for beauty than for aught else in the world; and that, in my case, it would be a great imprudence not to close at once with the highest bidder.'

'And what did *you* say, Gwendoline?' inquired her lover, gazing on her with passion, yet in wonderment—wrapped in a sort of charmed awe.

'He did not give me time to speak, Piers; but turning to the picture of our ancestor, Sir Ralph, he said: "The Tre-hernes have never been so poor as now save once, my dear, which was in this gentleman's time; who, as you see, had to take to beer, and backing his right hand against his left at cards; yet he contrived to marry an heiress, and thereby kept Bedivere Court in the family for a hundred and fifty years after him. Now, what that middle-aged profligate, in tattered clothes yonder, could manage to effect, lies easily enough, I fancy, within the reach of my daughter, Gwendoline." Nor, indeed, could

I deny that papa spoke truth in that, Piers.'

Self-conscious of the power of the beauty of which she spoke, she drew herself up to her full height, and her dark eyes flashed around her as though with the triumph they foresaw.

'But did you not tell him that you had promised yourself *to me?*' inquired her lover, not without some touch of dignity.

'I did not—because I saw he knew it already, Piers. Papa knows everything that can in any way affect himself, be sure of that. He knows what is good for us, since it also happens to be what is good for him. He did not use a single menace, nor even bid me never see you again. It is likely enough he understood you would be here to-night. He simply placed my position and yours before me, on the social map, just like a lesson in geography. "If you choose to marry this pleasant young sprig of nobility," said he, "you can of course do so. I will not even refuse my blessing, but I doubt whether you can live on that, or even pay his debts with it." '

' Gad, he is right there ! ' observed the Honourable Piers Mostyn ruefully.

' Of course he is right, Piers, or I would not have troubled you with these notes of his conversation. I love you, my darling; ah! *how* I love you, but as for our marriage '—

' Gwendoline, dearest · Gwendoline,' whispered the young man passionately, and passing his arm around her waist, ' let the world take its own way without us; for your sake I can be content to live on a crust ! Fly with me—to-night—to-morrow ! You shall stay with my old tutor and his wife until I can get the license. Nobody shall stop us; nothing shall turn me from you; you have only to say, " I will." '

For an instant—for a single instant— Gwendoline was silent: charmed with the glowing picture thus presented to her, her white cheek grew whiter, sicklied o'er by the pale hue of passion; she closed her eyes, as though to hide from herself that comely appealing face she so often saw, even in her dreams, but never so lover-like and fond as now; but the next moment she was herself again. 'No, Piers. We can neither of us afford this folly; or, at least,' added she, staying the vehement protestation upon the threshold of his lips with no trembling finger, 'I for my part cannot afford it. For argument's sake—or rather to avoid argument—let it be granted that *you* could undergo the sacrifice—that you, accustomed to luxury from your cradle, to extravagance and self-indulgence from your boyhood, could, for my sake, live, as you say, upon a crust; but for me, I am less simple in my tastes:

> Love in a hut with water and a crust,
> Is, Lord forgive us! cinders, ashes, dust.

Even a poet has had the good sense to see

that, Piers; and I am not a poet, nor
would be one even if I could. I too have
been brought up, if not in luxury, still
without lack of comforts, refinements, and,
of late years, I have tasted of the golden
water of life, the elixir of rank and wealth
—a Circe cup, as some call it—but which
is to me, I confess, most sweet and de-
lectable; nay, what is more, Piers, wealth,
or what wealth can buy, has become indis-
pensable to my happiness. Look at me—
you who called me Empress but a while
ago, and ask yourself the question—could
this girl live a life of poverty? No, Piers;
not even for your sake. If that love for
you, which I have acknowledged with no
niggard tongue, is to be lasting, it must be
put to no such test. In your heart of
hearts you will soon confess that I have
spoken for both of us—you will thank me
for not having permitted you to indulge a
generous but reckless impulse; but I am
content to bear the present blame myself;

to let the imputation of worldliness and selfish caution rest upon my own shoulders. You may call me calculating, but you can scarcely call me cold, my darling.'

He had unclasped his arm from around her waist, and over his finely chiselled features there had stolen, while she spoke, the same look of curiosity, almost of suspicion, that was already seen there once before—a look that seemed to say: 'This girl is not like other girls; I cannot fathom her;' but her last loving words evoked his smile again—and he had a very winning smile.

'No, Gwendoline; you are not cold,' said he fondly; 'it would be kinder to me if you were, since your view of our future is so unhopeful.'

'Do not despise me for my loving candour,' exclaimed the young girl suddenly: 'to tell you how I love you is the only luxury which is at present within my power, and now I have done with even

that. You must leave St Medards to-morrow, Piers. You must go home, or, at least,
far from this place.'

'Why so, my darling? Matters can be
no worse than they are now. Your father
understands our mutual position, and has
confidence—not ill-founded, as it seems—
in his daughter's prudence. I have been
here only four days, and seen you but
thrice.'

'Nevertheless, Piers, you must do as I
say, if you really wish to be one day able
to call me yours.'

'But how can my absence possibly
promote that end, Gwendoline?'

'Do not ask me, darling—do not press
me, I conjure you. Strive to believe,
rather, that the sight of you, the knowledge of your nearness to me, would be
more than I have strength to bear. Or,
if not so, credit me, Piers, when I tell you
that your absence *will* promote that end,
will bring us—slowly but surely—more

near to one another; will make me—it must, it shall, your wife at last!'

'And in the mean time, Gwendoline, is it possible I read you aright for once? Some other man is to be your husband.'

'Yes, Piers.'

A long silence fell between them: nothing was heard but the swift flow of the river, and the murmur of the fir-tree tops upon the crest of the opposite bank. Upon these, as they gently swayed in the moonlit air, they both fixed their eyes, not looking upon one another.

'And is this to be a one-sided arrangement?' inquired the young man presently, with a bitter laugh; 'or am I, too, to be free to wed?'

'*Free* do you call it!' exclaimed Gwendoline haughtily. 'Is it you, then, who have to make the sacrifice? Papa, indeed, must have spoken truth when he said men were all alike—harsh, selfish'—

'Dear Gwendoline, I ask pardon. It

is you, of course, who will have to suffer.
I do see that. But the proposition so took
me by surprise, I scarce knew what I
said.'

'Nay, you were right to speak your
thought, Piers. It is necessary that we
should thoroughly understand one another.
If you promise to remain single, I on the
other hand, will not impose unreasonable
terms upon you. You have been told, like
me, that your best chance in life—your
only prospect, indeed, it is like enough—
is to make a wealthy marriage. Well, so
be it. I have a definite plan, a plan that
will succeed, I feel; but if it fail—and it
may fail—I will release you at once from
your engagement. Or, if your debts should
so accumulate—although I trust to help
you *there*, Piers—as to necessitate— But
no; I cannot bear to think of that, my
darling; you will wait for me. You will
be patient, for the sake of your poor
wretched Gwendoline. For I *shall* be

wretched (ah, as you men can never guess)
until the time comes—until we shall be
both repaid for all.—You are not hating
me, darling, are you?—not despising me
for casting away all hope of happiness for
years, for your dear sake?'

'Nay, Gwendoline; I am all admiration: if your scheme seemed strange at
first, it is, I perceive, the only one that is
left to us. And yet I am lost in wonder
that you should have hit upon it. I have
always found women, even the wise ones,
so impracticable and full of sentiment.
Now, you have no nonsense about you of
that sort.'

'He does despise me,' thought Gwendoline, with a shudder. 'He would have
loved me better had I been a fool, like
other girls.' But she smiled upon him
fondly, as she answered: 'I am acting for
the best, my darling, and must fit myself
for the part I have to play as well as I can.
It is only the knowledge of your love that

will support me through it. I possess it—
do I not, Piers?—Yes, you say so, and I
believe you; but you can never love me as
I love you.'

Again he pressed her to his breast with
passionate warmth, and she felt that he
was hers once more: the risk she had run
of losing him altogether had been greater
than she had expected, but it was over
now. The dangerous subject had been
entered upon; she had skated over the
thin ice, and was safe; but it was better
not to venture near that perilous spot
again.

'You must leave me now, darling,'
said she, 'or that little fool of a waiting-
maid of mine will be coming out to look
for me. I will keep you well advised of
all that happens, but we must not meet
again at present. Remember, I am yours,
and yours only, for ever! How I long for
that dear day when you shall have the
right to call me so! Farewell—nay, not

another kiss, Piers—my own dear love, farewell.'

He leaped lightly into the skiff, and keeping it under the shadow of the terrace, and out of sight of the house, rowed rapidly away. Gwendoline watched him to the corner of the river-bend with hungry eyes, then sank down upon the arbour-seat in a paroxysm of tears and sobs.

'What a life is now before me,' gasped she, 'and without his smile to cheer it! My Piers, my Piers, how can I ever bear it! And was he to be "free to wed," he asked—no; a thousand times no. I would rather see him dead before my eyes! He was half-frightened at my plan, I know. When papa said he was glad to see that there was "no nonsense about me," it was different; I did not mind *his* words; but Piers thought ill of me for that, I know. What do they mean, these men, who bring us up to splendour and pleasure, who flatter us till there is no more simplicity of nature in us than in themselves, and then despise us for being what they have made us!'

Presently growing calmer, she put aside the tresses that had fallen over her drooping face, and gazed before her with eyes no longer tearful. 'How glad I am,' mused she, 'he did not press me for the details of my scheme. He spared me there, indeed, as did my father too. How I flushed up, I know, when papa said this morning: "There is nobody to marry you hereabouts, Gwendoline, who does not know a deal too much of the position of my affairs." But yet he had no suspicion of my plan. Even he has not the brains that I have; and much less Piers. And yet, ah, how I love dear Piers!' With a softened look on her proud face, and with her hands folded over her bosom, as though nourishing the fond thoughts that nestled there, Gwendoline moved slowly towards the house.

CHAPTER III.

A MOMENT OF TERROR.

GWENDOLINE's meeting with her lover had occupied more time than either of them had been aware of—it was not that their spoken words had been so many, but the thoughtful silences between them, the tender caresses, the lingering farewell, had prolonged their interview far into the night. Her maid Fanny was the only one of the household who had not retired to rest when her young mistress glided, ghost-like, up the garden-steps, and through the glass-door of the drawing-room. Notwith-standing that the population about St

Medards were, many of them, what are called a 'rough lot,' burglaries were quite unknown in the neighbourhood, and no shutters were ever fastened at Bedivere Court. Indeed, it would have been a work of considerable time, as well as toil, to close the whole house; and on that particular night, there was not a man in the place to do it. Butler, properly so called, there was none; and Sir Guy's own man, without whom he never moved, had accompanied his master to the county-town. Sir Guy had been accustomed to such ministrations all his life, and he was not the man, whatever his pecuniary difficulties, to retrench in any matter of personal comfort, far less to forego them. This absence, however, of all the male folk did leave the few inmates of the Court somewhat lonely and defenceless; and a young lady with more 'nonsense about her' than Gwendoline Treherne, might possibly have felt nervous. Waiting-maid Fanny, who had been sitting up by herself, with nothing but plain needle-work to absorb an erratic imagination, had been in fact for hours a prey to terror; in her ears, every creak of doors and rattle of windows had sounded like burglary with violence. It was infamous, thought she, of Sir Guy to have left them all so unprotected; and it would only serve him right if, when he returned home on the morrow, he should find the house pillaged and his daughter murdered; not that the selfish old gentleman would care much for the latter, so long as the plate was safe and his cigars untouched; nor perhaps even at all, since, if Miss Gwendoline was put out of the way, he would probably proceed to enjoy himself with less regard to respectability than even at present. What on earth should he want of poor Adolphe, making him sit behind the carriage over those long dreary miles of moorland, which the dear fellow hated so cordially, when his company and con-

versation would have been so unspeakably
consolatory to herself on an occasion like
the present ?   For Adolphe, although not
exactly in the heyday of youth (he was
five-and-forty at the very least, but had
learned from his master to look ten years
younger), had the most agreeable way with
him it was possible to conceive, and was
the most perfect gentleman imaginable ;
and how much nicer, thought Fanny,
would it be to be now listening to his
charming broken English, than to be sitting alone in the huge kitchen with only
the fading fire for her companion.

It was with a great sense of relief that
she at last heard the boudoir-bell ring, and
knew that her weary watch was finished.
The very sight of Miss Gwendoline--so
self-centered, self-reliant, calm—would be
assuring to her.   If she did not actually
love her young mistress, she had no cause
to dislike her, and she admired her beyond
all measure.   Not only as respected her

personal beauty, but also for her mental
qualities, which, though she herself could
not fathom them, Adolphe had assured her
were magnificent. 'She is too great to be
English' (he had informed her in a moment of enthusiasm): 'she ought to have
been born a Frenchwoman;' although, as
for her good looks, he had hastened to add,
he for his part preferred one with a rose on
her cheek, and a ravishing little smile
when one pats it tenderly *comme ça*. Women should not be too clever, for that was
almost certain to lead them into mischief.
Not that Miss Gwendoline's cleverness was
ever likely to do that, thought Fanny; for
in her it always took the shape of prudence
and caution. That very day, she had
been most unexpectedly taken into her
young mistress's confidence. Miss Gwendoline had told her that Mr Piers Mostyn
and herself, whom she had hitherto looked
upon as affianced lovers, would be hence-
forward strangers to one another, and that

that night's interview was to be their last.
It was, after all, only a foolish attachment,
she said, which must sooner or later end in
disappointment, and Sir Guy had been
doubtless right in peremptorily command-
ing her to put a stop to it. Fanny mar-
velled to hear her speak so calmly, but
never doubted her resolve, and the less so
inasmuch as Gwendoline had concluded
this dissertation upon her own affairs with
some excellent advice with respect to
Fanny's future government of herself in
love-matters, which she listened to with
much humility, though thinking in her
secret heart that she could never dismiss
dear Adolphe with such equanimity, even
though there was gray in one of his whiskers, and he was not the brother of a lord,
as Mr Piers Mostyn was.

But notwithstanding this proof of Miss
Gwendoline's confidence, the relation between the two girls was by no means
so intimate as often exists between mis-

tress and maid at their age. There was something about the former that was not haughtiness, and yet which kept her far more removed from her attendant than any implied difference of social position. Even now, that Fanny had been made the repository of so delicate a secret—which she did not know had only been revealed to her after all the reasons for and against such a revelation had been thoroughly weighed—she did not seem to herself to possess any hold over Miss Gwendoline, and scarcely even to be on a more familiar footing with her than heretofore. Even had not her thoughts been just then occupied with more pressing matter, it is probable she would not have ventured to speak to her young mistress of that interview which she knew had just taken place, and which had, for one of her simple and impulsive nature, a very engrossing interest. Gwendoline's steady eyes and passionless face in the glass before her—for Fanny was now

engaged in brushing the ample tresses of
' her young lady' preparatory to her re-
tirement for the night—would in any case
have forbidden any such allusion. Yet
Fanny had something to communicate
which must needs be uttered, at all hazards,
no matter what reflections of her philosophic mistress she might be breaking in
upon, for Fear is of all passions that which
stands the least upon ceremony, and may
so far indeed be said to be the most courageous. It was assuring, indeed, to see
Miss Gwendoline so calm and stately, unruffled by any idea so vulgar as possible
burglars; but then, thought Fanny, it will
be all the worse for me when I am dismissed
from her presence, and left to cower down
under the bed-clothes in my own room.
Still, she put off the proposition she was
about to make to the very last moment, when
the long brown locks hung in one broad
shining stream to the very ground, and the
ivory brush had fulfilled its task to the

uttermost. Then—'If you please, Miss Gwendoline, might I sleep on the sofa in your room to-night?' inquired she suddenly; 'I am so terribly frightened.'

'Frightened at what, you silly girl? Are you afraid, simply because Adolphe is not here to protect you, or because the wind is busy in the fir-wood?'

'No, miss, it's not only that; but I am quite certain there will be mischief here to-night, there have been such strange sounds while I have been waiting up for you; and just as your bell rang, I am almost certain I heard the great iron gate clang, and I am sure there is not wind enough to make it do that. If it had happened five minutes before, I should have even risked your displeasure by running out upon the terrace, and '—

'It was well you did not, girl,' interrupted Gwendoline severely; ' such foolish follies are only suitable to regale persons of your own class with. I am sorry to

refuse your request, but it is a most unreasonable one as you ought to know.   If
you are such a coward as you make out, go
and sleep with the cook or the housemaid.'

'*They* would be no protection, Miss
Gwendoline; indeed, I doubt whether
they would not be more frightened than
myself.'

'That is as you please, Fanny; but I
have a particular fancy for my own company to-night, and I mean to indulge it.—
What is that noise?'

'Lord have mercy upon us! it's the
hall-door banged, and they are in the house
already!' gasped the waiting-maid, clasp-
ing her hands.   'Oh, is Mr Piers Mostyn
really gone, ma'am; and must we all be
robbed and murdered?'

'Gone! Child, are you mad? Of course
he is gone.   Put the candles out, and remain as still as death, while I see what this
means.'   And Gwendoline, attired as she
was in her dressing-gown and slippers,

and with her long hair streaming over her
shoulders, passed quickly and noiselessly
from the room, which opened on to a corridor, from which she could look down
into the great hall itself. Though suspect-
ing that some intruder was in the house,
she did not even now entertain the idea of
burglary. Such a crime was not only, as
has been said, absolutely unknown in the
district—of which the leaving the front
door unlocked was proof enough—but Bedivere Court was the last house in the
county that a professional robber would
attempt. There was little in it indeed to
make it worth his while; and the risk, if
at least Sir Guy had been at home—and
his departure, quite suddenly resolved upon,
could scarcely have been known—was very
considerable. The baronet had firearms,
and his determination was beyond all
question. Indeed, it was rumoured, not
without justice, that he had used a pistol
with effect upon less occasion; and if

Gwendoline's heart throbbed with some excitement, as she leaned over the banisters and peered down into the gloom below, it was not with fear.

All was in shadow except the central space, upon which the moonbeams poured directly from the round north window that faced the door; and at first she could see nothing. But presently the figures of two men, motionless, and doubtless in the act of listening like herself, could be made out, standing at the foot of the broad staircase. There was a whispered colloquy, and then a sound as though they were taking their boots off; and in another minute they stood together on the bottom step, and it was plain they were coming up-stairs. Gwendoline stepped back into her own room, and without heeding her waiting-maid's terrified inquiries, passed through it with hasty steps into her father's bed-chamber, with which it had a door of communication. His pistol-box lay in its usual place by his bed's head, and she took from it one of the choice and highly orna-mented little weapons it contained, ascer-tained that it was loaded, capped it, and dropped it into the pocket of her dressing-gown. She hid the box, and returned to Fanny, who had fallen on her knees, and was listening at the keyhole of the outer door, which her young mistress had not omitted to make fast. Gwendoline had fewer ornaments of price than most girls in her position call their own. She did, however, possess one diamond necklace, the gift of a godmother, who, in bestowing it upon her, had considered herself absolved from all obligations, temporal and spirit-ual; and this she thrust, case and all, into the bosom of her dressing-gown, leaving the jewel-drawer with the rest of its con-tents half open; then, for the first time, the hushed wail of her terrified attendant, imploring her to tell her what she had seen, and who was in the house, attracted her attention.

'Cease that whining, girl!' said she imperatively. 'Whoever these men are, you must not appear afraid of them. Look at me; do I seem afraid? And yet these jewels are not yours, but mine.'

Standing in the moonlight, with one hand in the pocket of her dress, and the other raised as if for silence, her noble features no paler than usual, and not less calm, except for a certain twitching of the nostril, which spoke of insulted dignity— of angry pride rather than of any other feeling—she certainly did not look afraid. But Fanny was much too prostrated by nervous terror to pluck comfort now from even her mistress.

'Then they are really robbers, are they?' answered she. 'God help us!'

'I don't know whether they are robbers

or not,' was the calm reply; ' but they are
certainly here for no good. I saw them as
they were coming upstairs, and the moonlight shone upon an iron ring that was
round one man's ankle. They are most
likely, therefore, convicts escaped from
Dartmoor.'

CHAPTER IV.

WHICH EXHIBITS SOME TRAITS OF CHARACTER.

At this moment, the handle of the door was cautiously tried from the outside.

'Who is there?' cried Gwendoline, in tones whose very distinctness might have shown to a keen observer that they were the result of effort, but which at least spoke of self-possession.

There was no answer to this inquiry.

'Unbolt the door, girl!' continued Gwendoline resolutely.

'What! let them in?' ejaculated Fanny, to whose weaker nature procras-

tination seemed something akin to safety.
' No, no ! '

' Then *I* will do it,' said her mistress.
She swept across the room like a stage-
queen (perhaps she was in some sort re-
hearsing for the part she had set herself to
play, when the audience without should be
admitted), drew back the bolt, and threw
the door wide open. Never had oaken plank
divided persons more wholly different in
appearance than were those two, whom she
now confronted, from herself. Imagine,
on the one side, the haughtiest of fair
women, youthful, beautiful, and in an attire
in which those of her sex and condition
are only seen by their most intimate female
friends; and, on the other, two outcasts,
ragged, wayworn, and yet with a scowl
upon their haggard faces, which recked
little indeed of rank and station, and boded
as ill as any royal tyrant's frown to whom-
soever should cross their wishes. Although
each had found means to exchange his

prison-clothes, and, as it seemed, with some scarecrow of the fields, Gwendoline's quick glance had not misled her as to their true character. On the ankle of each was a strong iron ring, about which, whether for concealment, or to prevent its rubbing against the limb, a rag was loosely twisted. They were both ill-looking, desperate-eyed fellows enough, and the more assimilated in ferocious expression by a three days' growth of bristly hair upon lip and chin. But even here Nature had stamped beyond erasure some points of difference. The shorter of the two, though they were both tall men, was by far the most truculent-looking. For an instant the spectacle thus suddenly presented to his gaze of transcendent female beauty and stateliness, where he had expected to meet cringing terror, took him with some surprise, and he lowered the point of his rude weapon — which was but a stake plucked from some sheepfold—at the sight of it; but the next

moment, as though resenting that involuntary tribute of respect, he raised it again,
and shook it in Gwendoline's face. 'We
want no play-acting here, young woman,
nor any of your d—d airs and graces. I
heard you just now telling your wench
there that she was not to appear to be
afraid of us; but she *is* afraid—and small
blame to her—and so are you.'

'If you heard that, sir,' said Gwendoline scornfully, and keeping her eyes
fixed upon the ruffian's face, notwithstanding that his weapon was held within an
inch of them, 'you also heard me say that
I, for my part, was not afraid. Nor am I.
What is it you want here, man?'

'Well, several things. Money to begin
with; jewels, such as I see yonder; and
food and drink above all.'

'Money, I have none,' said Gwendoline
firmly; 'or, at least, what will seem none
to gentlemen of your ambition. There
lies my purse, however.'

'There must be more than that in a house like this,' cried the villain impatiently.—'Here, *you* with your eyes half out of your head'—and he turned sharply round upon the wretched Fanny, who was literally petrified with fear—'is this sleek young mistress of yours telling us lies or not? If so, you had better not try the same game, I promise you.'

'Indeed, dear gentlemen, we have no money,' gasped the waiting-maid imploringly. 'Sir Guy is from home.'

Gwendoline flashed upon her a glance as of forked lightning, yet not so swiftly but that her persecutor caught sight of it.

'Ah,' said he contemptuously, 'you may spare yourself the trouble of all that, miss. We are not to be imposed upon even by a clever one like you. We have been watching about here all day in the wood above the house yonder, and know exactly how matters stand. We saw Sir Guy, if that's the master's name, take hisself off, and his man with him, this afternoon; and more than that, my fine lady, we saw *your* young gentleman slip down the river so quietly not half an hour ago, which was a pretty time o' night, by the way, in my opinion, for a perfect lady to be courted in a garden arbour—not that Bob and I would have cared two straws, only we were so deuced sharp set for our supper.'

The man who spoke these words, a waif and stray of society from his birth, had been thrown from early youth among dangerous company on sea and land, and had fought his way among them to a bad eminence through many a bloody brawl and desperate conflict, and yet, perhaps, he had never been nearer to death than he was that moment. If Gwendoline's features maintained their outward calm, it was only by means of indrawn breath and tight clenched teeth; her hand clutched the weapon in the pocket of her robe with feverish eagerness, while her eyes fixed

themselves upon the ruffian's mocking face
with a hatred that had no longer contempt
to mitigate it.

'And yet, if I kill this reptile,' murmured she, 'my whole plan must fail.'

'What are you muttering now?' inquired the ruffian savagely. 'It seems to
me you are just the obstinate sort of fool
as gets her brain-pan knocked in on little
occasions like the present. I shall have to
take *you* in hand myself, I see.' As he
stepped towards her, Gwendoline withdrew
her hand from her pocket. She could not
trust it there if he should lay a finger on
her—and yet the thought that her scheme
of life should be wrecked by this audacious
scum was even more terrible to endure.

'You have no more money in the house,
you say,' said he, standing close beside
her; 'have you no more jewels than those
which we have already got?' She confronted him haughtily as ever, and pointing
mechanically, to give corroboration to her

words, to the very spot where the diamonds lay concealed, she answered: 'I have not.'

'And the plate, where does Sir Guy keep his plate?'

'In the pantry, in an iron chest, of which he has the key,' returned Gwendoline.

'This won't do, miss,' ejaculated the ruffian with a horrible oath, and he seized her roughly by the wrist.

'Stop, Dick,' cried the other man, speaking for the first time. 'Hands off; I can't have that. The young lady is speaking the truth, and what's the use of bullying? Besides, what could we do with plate even if we found it. We have got the gewgaws and the money; let us now have food and drink, for I feel as famished as a wolf.' The man called Dick threw sullenly from him the plump white wrist which still retained the mark of his cruel clutch.

'You were always a fool, Bob, where a

woman was concerned; but this one at least is not worth while for us two to quarrel over; only I don't lose sight of her while in this house, no, not for an instant.—It is you who shall be our waiting-maid at table; and I shall keep my eye upon you, my fine lady, lest you should take a fancy to drug our drink. It would do you all the good in the world to have a master like me for a week or two. I'd tame you, my young tigress.'

For the first time throughout this terrible scene, Gwendoline fairly shuddered. Pride of lineage, pride of position, haughtiness even of character itself, must needs succumb sooner or later, if the necessity be extreme. The contemptuous stoicism of high breeding—but a faint shadow, after all, compared with the stubborn immobility of the thieving, lying savage—requires for its foundation the possession of what is vulgarly denominated the upper hand. As in some general overturn of

society, a Robespierre becomes as calmly
terrible as any nobleman of twenty times
transmitted title, who could scatter his
lettres de cachet broadcast, and with tranquil
face immure for life the *canaille* who aspired
to be his foes, with one stroke of his pen;
so in particular cases, where something
that is not accustomed to be Might, suddenly becomes so (and, as is usual, with a
vengeance), even the supremest aristocratic
contempt of it is apt to break down—if
the pressure be only sharp enough. The
scornful demeanour may, indeed (and often
does), remain; but the victories of de-
portment, although by no means despica-
ble, are more effectual on canvas than in
real life. Thus Gwendoline Treherne,
although still a glorious picture of contemptuous dignity—and that bold show
stood her in good stead—had, in fact, for
the moment succumbed before the insolent
superiority of this familiar ruffian. Involuntarily, the vision of an impossible life

with this brutal wretch, whose grasp she still felt upon her wrist, as her master, flashed upon her mind, and chilled her with its horror.

'You have the keys, Fanny,' said she in a voice that all her resolution could not keep free from tremor; 'let these men have food and wine.'

'Ay, and my fine lady for company also,' insisted ruffian Dick. 'She shall sit at the head of the table, if she pleases, but at our feast she shall be: next to drink, and one or two other little weaknesses, I enjoy the taming of tigresses above all things.—And besides, Bob,' added he, as his companion seemed again about to interfere, 'who knows but there may be an alarm-bell in the house, which this young lady, if left here to herself, would be just the one to pull with a will.'

But poor frightened Fanny was by no means in a condition to undertake any housekeeping arrangements whatever; it

was as much as she could do to accompany
her young mistress, and point out to her,
with trembling limbs and hysterical sobs,
where this and that was to be found, so
that Bob and Dick were in fact provided
for by Gwendoline's own hands; and she
stood beside them while the hungry
wretches ate and drank their fill — as
strange a waiting-maid as ever served still
stranger guests. As the repast progressed,
the more silent of the two men grew talk-
ative, while the other in his turn kept
silence, the good cheer seeming only to
make him more morose and grim.

'I am sorry that we trouble you so
much, young lady,' said the former, addressing Gwendoline with some show of
respect; 'but we have been near two days
without food, and know not when we may
get another meal.'

As Gwendoline did not vouchsafe one
word of reply, Fanny, who really felt a
kindliness towards this man (as being evi-

dently the milder of the two, and who had more than once interfered to check the rudeness of his companion), suggested that they should take some provisions with them.

'Right, little wench!' cried Dick; 'but my fine lady shall cut it for us, and not you.—Nay, Bob, you may be served as you will, but for my part I like to be waited on by the quality.' As Gwendoline took the bread-knife, without a word, and proceeded to cut some slices, one more acquainted with the fine arts than the present company might well have likened her to Judith in the tent of Holofernes. Although this parallel did not occur to the observant Dick, the expression of her face did not escape him. 'Look at her how she cuts the loaf,' he said; 'how much rather would she be carving you and me with that big knife, than bread to help us on our way.—Be quiet, you,' roared he, interrupting himself suddenly. — 'What noise was that outside?'

The wind had ceased, so that sounds could be heard through the night-air from far; and it was not without intention that Gwendoline had been clumsy with the wooden plate, and made it clatter upon the clothless board. She had caught the distant fall of horses' feet, and so—although less distinctly—had her persecutor. The two men started from their seats, and listened eagerly; not like hunted hares, but as wild beasts tracked to their lair, they stood with savage eager looks, and each with knife in hand.

'Have you boats here?' cried the shorter ruffian fiercely.

'O yes, sir,' answered Fanny eager-ly; 'there is one under the terrace, and'—

'I spoke to *you*,' interrupted Dick, turning upon Gwendoline a look of concentrated rage. 'And you shall answer me, or I will hang for it'—

'Oh, answer him, Miss Gwendoline; pray, answer him,' pleaded Fanny piteously.

'I will show you where the boat lies, if that is what you want,' said Gwendoline.

'Be quick, then,' answered the ruffian. 'But, first, I will hear both of you swear by Heaven that you will say we have gone over the hill yonder, and not by water.'

'O yes, sir, we will promise to do that. I swear to tell them what you wish.'

'And you—you she-devil,' exclaimed Dick, pointing at Gwendoline with his knife, 'will you swear too, or not?'

Gwendoline did not speak. Once more her hand had sought the pocket of her dressing-gown.

'Well, the boat first then,' cried the ruffian impatiently, 'and we will have the promise afterwards.'

Gwendoline led the way into the garden at a rapid pace. The two men followed her; but Fanny's limbs fairly refused
to carry her.

'Will it not be better to make both
safe, Bob?' whispered Dick to his companion hoarsely. 'Dead men tell no tales,
nor even dead women.'

'No, no; I will not have it,' answered
the other with a shudder: 'there is blood
enough on our hands already.'

'There will be more on mine, if my
fine lady does not promise what I ask her,'
muttered the other to himself; and both
hurried down to the river's edge. Beneath
the stone arbour was a boat-house, with a
punt in it, and Gwendoline led them to it.

'Is there none but that?' inquired
Dick suspiciously. 'You must have a skiff
here, surely.'

'The gentleman you saw to-night has
taken it,' returned Gwendoline quietly.

'Curse him and you!' answered the

ruffian passionately.—'Get in, Bob.—Now,
mark you, my lady, I have no scruples
like my friend yonder, and upon your
answer to my next question will depend
whether you ever see that sweetheart of
yours again or not. If it be "Yes," then
well and good; but if it be "No," that
word will be your last;' and as though he
had known of the weapon that she had
hidden in her robe, he grasped both her
wrists in one huge hand, so that she was
powerless, and with the other he put the
naked knife to her white throat. 'Do you
swear, as you hope for Heaven,' said he, in
a fierce whisper, 'to tell those curs who
are at our heels that we have gone over
yonder hill an hour ago?'

She felt the sharp blade press against
her skin.

'Quick, quick!' cried he through his
clenched teeth.

'I promise,' whispered she — 'I
swear.'

'Then you may live to trouble your sweetheart yet,' said the ruffian with a brutal laugh, and he leaped into the punt as his companion pushed it swiftly from the shore.

There was not a moment to lose. Lights were visible, and voices heard, from the house, as Gwendoline hastily returned thither. An officer and four troopers, armed to the teeth, had dismounted in the court-yard, and the former was even then engaged in cross-examining Fanny, while some other terrified domestics stood by with greedy ears.

'It is strange how they could have gone by the moor,' he said with perplexity; 'we must have surely come across them that way ourselves '—

'They are not gone by the moor,' interrupted Gwendoline, gliding in with her usual stateliness, and speaking in a voice whose firmness strongly contrasted with her maid's hysterical and broken speech.

'They are gone down the river, and not five minutes ago.'

' O Miss Gwendoline, and we promised not to tell ! ' exclaimed the faithful Fanny.

' *You* promised, you coward, but not I ! ' answered her mistress contemptuously. 'They have taken the punt, sir, in which they can make little way. There is a four-oar in the large boat-house, if your men can row, in which you can overtake them before they have gone a mile.'

' That is excellent, madam ; we will be off at once.—But, forgive me, your neck is bleeding. These ruffians have surely never dared to offer you any violence ! '

' One put a knife to my throat, sir, and grazed it—that is all,' answered Gwendoline calmly. 'It was the shorter of our two visitors.'

' And by far the most dangerous, madam. They have killed a warder between them in making their escape, and will certainly both be hung ; but the man you speak of is the most ferocious ruffian that even Dartmoor ever held. Now your peril is over, I may tell you that I am as surprised as delighted to find you alive.'

All this was said as the party were hurrying through the garden to the other end of the terrace, where a larger boathouse than that beneath the arbour was situated.

' The trooper who remains with the horses will be your protection until we return,' continued the officer; 'although, of course, there is no further peril to be apprehended. I am glad indeed '—and he courteously raised his cap—' that it has fallen to my lot to be able to afford some assistance to Miss Treherne, of whom all the world '—

' Your boat is ready, sir,' said Gwendoline coldly; ' this is no time for compliment; and I shall reserve my thanks until you return with those infamous wretches as your prisoners.'

' I trust to give a good account of them shortly, madam,' answered the young lieutenant, not a little abashed.—' You two there, take the oars; and you other, sit in the stern with all four carbines, and keep a good look-out. If they do not surrender, take good aim, and fire.— Give way, men ! '

The boat shot out at a pace that must needs bring them up with the object of their pursuit in a few minutes.

Gwendoline remained upon the river terrace with one or two women-servants, the latter garrulous enough, she herself wrapt in thought.

' How glad I am,' mused she, ' that I never used the pistol. My plan of life must else have altogether failed. He could never have understood the necessity for such an action, nor forgiven me—except in his cold formal way—though Piers would have loved me none the less.—Well, there is one advantage in this night's work, that it will be sure to bring them over from Glen Druid to-morrow, and throw us still more together.—That is something I shall have to thank yon hateful villain for, as well as for this flesh-wound, of which I must make the most! He has bruised my wrist, too, with his brutal gripe; and I shall be a most interesting young woman for many a day to come! If he had only held them but a little less firmly he would have been a dead man by this.—Hark! '

The silence of the autumn night was broken by a musket-shot, of which the echoes seemed to leap from bank to bank from far down stream; and then another, and yet another shot.

' Perhaps, he is a dead man now,' said Gwendoline, ' and his fellow-ruffian with him. I hope it is so. It would be much better that the affair should end, so far as they are concerned.'

CHAPTER V.

DR GISBORNE.

THE young lieutenant of dragoons brought back no prisoners to Bedivere Court that night, but took the bodies of two dead men into St Medards instead. The convicts had refused to surrender, and had been shot down accordingly. ' It was the best thing that could possibly have happened to them,' as everybody said. Of course it would have been a more exciting course for the present narrator to have preserved at least ruffian Dick alive; with his vengeance for her broken promise hanging throughout three volumes over

the head of the proud and lovely Gwendoline; but to Truth even Sensation must be
sacrificed, and the incident of the burglary
has been only mentioned just as it really
occurred, in order to illustrate the character of her who may now be literally termed
our heroine, since she did in fact, after that
strange night's work, become the cynosure
of admiring eyes throughout the country
round. Her presence of mind, her noble
demeanour under such trying circumstances, and especially her resolution, under pain of death itself, to withhold a
promise, that on one of her blue blood
would of course have been more binding
than the oath of any middle-class personage, were, thanks to Fanny's communicat-
iveness, the theme of a hundred pens,
notwithstanding that her mistress abhorred
such vulgar publicity, and discouraged it
to the uttermost. The sympathy, indeed,
of the whole district for this beautiful and
heroic young lady was so marked and ex-

tensive (for even the ratepayers felt grateful to her for having rid them of Bob and
Dick), that Sir Guy had almost begun to
hope that it might assume the form (and
dimensions) of a service of plate. 'In case
it should take that pleasing shape, my
dear,' was his characteristic advice to his
daughter, 'it will be necessary, before
accepting it, to consider whether it is
worth our while to do so; to count the
cost in the most practical manner, to consider whether the gain would be of such a
magnitude as to outweigh all other con-
siderations—such as that loss of *prestige*
which almost always accompanies the ac-
ceptance of any public gift. If the sub-
scription for the article in question—let us
say a service of gold plate—should reach
five thousand pounds, my dear, I should
recommend you to accept it; but if it fall
short of that amount, I should consider it
my duty to decline it, in your name; and
to add, that I should not have permitted

you to take it, had it cost fifty thousand.'

Sir Guy had established with his daughter that relation of perfect confidence which is so often wanting between parent and child. His frankness in the statement of his views to her on every point was always complete. His character, indeed, was naturally candid; he had no false shame—nor, in fact, shame of any kind; and it was commonly agreed of Sir Guy Treherne, that though he might not be without his faults, and even his vices, you saw the worst of him at once, and could never complain that you had been imposed upon by appearances. Much, we do not deny, should have been forgiven to the last male descendant of an ancient family, who was also a baronet, and who, although far from rich, had, by judiciously spending every shilling upon himself, contrived, throughout his life, to deny himself nothing in the way of luxury: so far as that went, there were as many allowances to be made

for him as for the most spoiled darling of
Fortune. But still, though he was no dis-
sembler, Sir Guy had a certain pleasing
bonhommie about him—or could have, when
he pleased—which had all the effect of the
most finished hypocrisy, at a third of the
cost. With satire of the sharpest at his
command, he never intentionally wounded
a fellow-creature's feelings—not that he
gave himself the least trouble to avoid it,
but that his fine tact (the result of long
training in the school of manners) steered
him always clear. His air was concili-
atory, and without condescension; his
smile, though stereotyped, was like the
approbation of a seraph. His attire was
always faultless: not even his daughter
had ever caught Sir Guy in his dressing-
gown. His wig was such a marvel of art,
that it was a matter of doubt, even among
his neighbours, as to whether he wore his
own hair. His small delicate hands—
which trembled a little, if you were rude

enough to watch them narrowly—showed
no traces of that gout the tortures of which
at times made him believe in the possibility
of a Gehenna. Upon the whole, he suggested some highly executed automaton,
which gracefully expresses almost every
human feeling without possessing it, and it
is not, therefore, to be wondered at that it
was the universal opinion, that whatever
his shortcomings—by which phrase the
absence of morality, religion, and all the
unselfish sentiments were indicated—Sir
Guy Treherne was pre-eminently a gentleman.

Even the one vulgar virtue which, in
its vulgar form, Sir Guy condescended to
possess, and, when necessary, to exhibit—
that of personal courage—was dashed with
artificiality. He would have fought his
enemy or his friend across a pocket-hand-
kerchief, and never changed colour at the
measured 'One, two, three' of the signal-
ler; but he shrank from illness, and still

more from the approach of death. He
used to openly confess that, had he been
rich enough, he would have maintained a
family physician—'Half-a-dozen of them,'
he was won't to add, 'rather than one
domestic chaplain.' And even as it was,
he liked to see his doctor pretty often. It
was one of the many blessings for which
Sir Guy used to express himself grateful—
for he was polite, if he failed to be winning, even to Providence itself—that there
was a most excellent physician at St
Medards. Dr Gisborne was an accomplished and highly educated gentleman, a
philosopher, a man of great and varied
experience in human affairs, and a most
agreeable companion; but what capped
all, in the baronet's estimate of his merits,
was, that he 'understood' Sir Guy—by
which, of course, he meant that he understood his constitution, knew which particular spring was likely to give way, and
patched it up, so that the sorely tried

apparatus of his system (which had been an excellent one in its time) was kept going with as few break-downs as possible.

Dr Gisborne and himself were in reality of the same age—namely, sixty-four, and neither of them looked to be within ten years of it. But what Art had done for the baronet in this respect, Nature had accomplished for the physician, so that the equality was only superficial: in external appearance they were both fine old trees; but one was a heartless shell, the other was still green and vigorous to the core. With all his experience of mankind, Dr Gisborne had still retained a certain simplicity. He was an old bachelor; yet the gambols of a child could afford him pleasure, and the beauty of a woman touched him with a certain reverence. His devotion to Gwendoline, for instance, was so chivalric and complete, that when Sir Guy, during that conversation with his daughter of which we have spoken, had remarked: ' There is

no one to marry you hereabouts,' he had
added, with characteristic pleasantry—
'unless you mean to take Dr Gisborne.'
Gwendoline had certainly no intention of
doing that; and yet the physician was,
next to Piers, the man who had for her the
greatest attraction. Sir Guy had told him
truly that she had once observed that Dr
Gisborne was the man most worth talking
to she had ever met; and the physician
was not perhaps insensible to flattery from
such lips as Gwendoline Treherne's. At
all events, he always put forth his best
conversational powers to please her, nor
ever balked her wishes, no matter into
what channels she might choose to lead his
talk; and he liked her none the less that
some of them were strange ones for the
belle of a London season to select. Dr
Gisborne was not a wit, and at a modern
dinner-table he would have made no great
figure; in that rapid interchange of jest
and fancy which forms the charm of to-

day's entertainments, he would have taken
no part; his fort was not so much conversation as monologue. He was a *raconteur*
of the very first water, but of the old
school, and would have bored the present
generation in Pall Mall to extremity. But
to Gwendoline much that he had to say
was not only attractive in a very high de-
grée, but, as she felt, was a lesson of life:
she gleaned from him the experience of
threescore years, and carefully garnered
so much of it as seemed likely to be useful
to her. The study of humanity was itself
interesting to her, as it is to all persons
not wholly inane and frivolous, and the
more so because the results of it were
practical. She asked him for no advice.
He only saw in her an attentive and
beautiful listener. No woman could have
ever suffered harm from Dr Gisborne's
teaching—but then he was wholly unaware
that Gwendoline Treherne was his pupil at
all. Perhaps, when launched upon the

great sea of his experience, he suffered at
times his memory to carry him too much
whither it would; not, indeed, that he
ever forgot whom he was addressing, in
the sense that Madame Propriety would
understand it—but his narrations were so
wholly pagan, that they might have been
recorded by some savage chief, supposing
it were possible to find one with whom
truth was any object. To Dr Gisborne,
all such matters were the mere outside of
life; to his perception, the great scheme of
Fatherly Beneficence still existed, notwithstanding that he had mixed with a society
in foreign parts where people were not
only backbiters, but actually devoured one
another. To Gwendoline, these strange
experiences of her old friend and neighbour only corroborated the view of Life
which her own bringing-up had already
formed for her: it showed to her, in its
most favourable aspect, a landscape set

more or less with (artificial) flowers, bor-
dered and terminated by the grave.

Dr Gisborne's reminiscences were of
course not exclusively cannibal; but those
which he liked best to dwell upon, as
Gwendoline to listen to, were undoubtedly
such as dealt with the most striking—and
often the most terrible of human facts.
Those who war against Sensation — a
cuckoo-note of invective, however, which
certainly seems to afford them extraordinary
pleasure—are indeed fighting, if not against
human nature itself, against all the more
robust and intelligent of mankind, and are
as likely to succeed as those who advocate
raw salads in preference to those prepared
according to the famous poetical recipe.
It is not really that they are more delicate
in their tastes than other people, but only
that they are more ignorant and feeble.
They boast of their weak stomachs, but it
is not their digestive organs which are at

fault, so much as their mental powers. To such bread-and-butter folks, everything out of their own little round of life is toast and caviare, with a dash of lemon; and their private opinion of *Lear* and *Othello* would be found quite as unfavourable, if any one took the trouble to ask for it, as the last railway novel with a murder in it, and the illustration of that attractive incident upon its yellow cover. The talk of Dr Gisborne would certainly have sometimes made the flesh of these good gentry to creep—caused them to feel more 'goosey' than even nature had intended them to be. It might be easily imagined that the burglary at Bedivere Court would rather have encouraged than otherwise that sort of converse in which the doctor and Gwendoline both delighted. But talk will often fly off at a tangent to apparently quite alien topics, and so it was in this case. Dr Gisborne had been one of the first at St Medards to hear of the incident, and had ridden over early in the morning, and obtained the details from his favourite's own lips, as they walked together in the garden.

'Of course you are none the worse for it all, my dear,' said he admiringly. 'Give me your pretty white hand again—pulse tranquil, skin without a touch of fever; that's well. It would have given some girls fits for life.'

'I couldn't afford to have fits for life,' observed Gwendoline demurely; 'but I really was a little frightened at one time, when the gentleman who was called Dick remarked that he should like to be my master, and break my spirit. Then, I own, I felt cold all over.'

'That was curious,' said the doctor musing. 'One would have thought when he seized you by the wrist—upon which the brute has left his mark, by-the-by, I see—that that would have been the supreme moment of terror.'

'No,' said Gwendoline simply; 'I did not feel so frightened then.'

She did not mention that she had had a loaded pistol in the pocket of her dressing-gown even to her friend the doctor; she had discussed that matter in her mind in the mean time, and decided upon silence.

'Well, it was a most striking experience,' said the physician, regarding her from head to foot with great approbation: he had known her for many a year, and was far prouder of her than Sir Guy himself had ever been. 'That fellow Dick must have been as bold as Jack Cade, to dare to talk so to such a queen.'

'A queen; nay, my dear doctor,' returned Gwendoline smiling; 'but that was not *his* opinion, since he called me a tigress.'

'Yet that was strange too,' replied the physician gravely. 'He, of course, meant the expression as a compliment in its way. With folks of his stamp, who belong to the family of the great *Carnivora*, it is the tigress who *is* queen. I always thought you myself as like the pictures of Catharine Alexiewna as a good girl can be to a very bad woman.'

'The Empress of Russia, was she not?' said Gwendoline, not without a thrill of pride, as she reflected that three such different men as Piers Mostyn, ruffian Dick, and Dr Gisborne should have thus, within twelve hours, all paid their tributes of admiration to her imperial bearing.

'Yes, she was empress,' returned the doctor contemptuously; 'but she was more fit to have kept a public-house. You know I only care for Nature's empresses, such as you, my dear.'

'Yes, you are a true republican, I believe,' observed Gwendoline thoughtfully; 'you take people for what they are worth, and so forth; your motto is, "Handsome is as handsome does;" and your arms— But there, you despise arms of course.'

'Well, my arms are a pestle and mortar, you know,' replied the doctor smiling.

'And you have been all over the world, and seen life in all its phases,' continued Gwendoline, still musing.

'Just so, my dear; I have seen a great many men and cities, but I prefer my lodgings at St Medards. In that respect, I am like an old gentleman whom my grandfather, when quite a boy, was in the habit of seeing—a small but very neatly dressed personage of fourscore years and more, who had three very stately daughters. "For my part," he was wont to say, "I am quite content and comfortable as I am now; but these ladies here, they can never forget that their father was once Lord Protector of Great Britain." I am quite of Mr Richard Cromwell's opinion— for the little old gentleman was no less— but I am afraid, my dear, you side with his daughters. Well, that is the way of all the women-folk; they are caught with a glittering fly at all seasons; but I hope you will not henpeck me, my dear, as the Misses Cromwell did their papa.'

'And yet, doctor,' said Gwendoline thoughtfully, and without taking notice of her companion's last remarks, ' you have an uncommon reverence for some persons who would be nothing but for the position they have inherited.'

'My dear Gwendoline, if you and I were in the House of Commons together,' observed the doctor with some severity, 'and you had indulged in such a remark, there would have been cries of "Name, name," from somebody; but being a young lady, your little assertions need no corroboration.'

'Now, that is the only thing which makes me doubt your sincerity,' exclaimed Gwendoline; 'you are always ruffled when anybody questions this republicanism of yours.'

'Not at all, my dear, not at all; but I think it is as important to stick to truth in speaking of matters of opinion as in speaking of matters of fact. I am interested, I own, in the maintenance of the principle which you have epitomized in your phrase of " Handsome is as handsome does." I think it very much for the public weal that all things should be taken at their true value, and not at a fancy price ; and as, in these parts at least, I am generally in a minority of one, I do not like to be misrepresented (and especially by Miss Gwendoline Treherne), so that even what little weight my influence might possess is thereby counteracted, or even thrown into the opposite scale. Now, what was it, my dear, which caused you to say that I pay reverence to people on account of the accident of birth ? '

' Well, doctor, you know that we could scarcely tear you away from Llandulph, the day of our pic-nic, merely because of that imperial tombstone—'

' Oh, that was it, was it ? ' interrupted

the physician smiling. ' Well, I do plead guilty there. But the fact is that, in the first place, I have no objection even to emperors, when their line is extinct; and secondly, my admiration was extorted by the vicissitude of the family in question, rather than by its quondam eminence. The tombstone (if you remember) was erected to the memory of a simple country gentleman, who had married the daughter of one William Ball, Esq. of Hadley; but he had a very curious name. It was Theodore Palæologus—direct descendant of a race that had given eight emperors to Constantinople. He died two hundred years ago, it is true; but the inscription says he left three sons; and yet, when— the other day—a deputation came over here from Greece, in hopes of finding a descendant of the great Constantine fool enough to be their king, no more could be heard of the family than of the old Derby Finderns—and indeed even less.'

'I don't know about the Finderns,' said
Gwendoline, not displeased to lead her
companion from a topic on which she had
nothing in common with him—for as there
were few more devoted to the show and
glitter of life than herself, so there was
none more contemptuous of them than the
philosophic physician; the one might have
been likened to Semiramis, the other to
Aristides ; only in this case Aristides exhibited the anomaly of a republican anti-
quary: even the memory of a Tyrant
became respectable in Dr Gisborne's eyes
after a sufficient number of centuries.

'Well, the story of the Finderns is
very curious. I only know it from Burke's
account ; but it always struck me as an
interesting illustration of the vanity of
what is called "position," and especially
of that ludicrous provincial branch of it
which is called a "position in the county."
The Finderns of Findern were a great
county family from Edward I.'s time;

the old local records are full of them. Yet,
when Sir Bernard went down there, upon
one of his wild-goose chases—pedigree-
hunting, poor creature—he could not find
one single relic of the old race; not a
stone seemed to have belonged to them—
not even in the church or churchyard.
"We have no Finderns here," said a vil-
lager; "but we have the Findern flowers;"
and he led the visitor to a field which
still showed dim traces of terraces and
foundations. "There," observed he,
pointing to a bank of garden-flowers grown
wild—"there are the Findern flowers,
brought by Sir Geoffrey from the Holy
Land; and do what we will, they will
never die." That seems to me very touch-
ing,' observed the doctor pathetically;
'although, of course, the poor Finderns
never did anything worth speaking of, or
which anybody would care to remember.
For that matter, indeed, the old houses
that *are* remembered—the oldest houses in

the world—have little to boast of in the way of merit. In a long line of ancestors, it would seem strange if some were not more or less distinguished. And yet how seldom is this the case! The Montmorencies, the Tremouilles, the Rochefoucaulds, have, after all, had but one representative. Of all the grandees of Spain, how many have made it worth the world's while to remember them? What have the most ancient nobility in the world—the Milesians—done for human kind? What have the Hapsburgs?—among whom there has been but one with a genius, and that only for aggrandizing his own family. Or that ducal family of Arcot—the most venerable in the world, as we are told, simply because it can *trace* its descent up to the Deluge (thereby saving you and me the trouble of tracing ours some distance for ourselves)—what did they ever do, beyond spending a good deal of money in such idle researches? The whole system of

hereditary nobility is contrary to fact, as
well as to philosophy. It is the new blood,
and not the old, which enriches the world.
—You smile, my dear Gwendoline, because you see me curveting on my hobby,
but it is a matter of fact and common
sense, and lies within your own observation. Who is it, for instance, who does the
most and best service in this very district?
Which are the more active for usefulness
and for good? the old families or the new?
Look at that new-comer and parvenu—as
all the old gentry hereabouts but your
father (who has better sense) are accustomed to call him—Mr Ferrier of Glen
Druid for instance. What an impetus has
he given to everything that is worth
pushing on, above ground and below it, as
well as on sea! I tell you that our labour-
ers in the fields, our workmen in the mines,
our fishermen at St Medards, have better
reason to praise the wise benevolence that
enriches without enslaving them, than all

the feudal patronage to which they have
been accustomed for these hundreds of
years.'

The enthusiastic philosopher paused
for sheer want of breath, not at all because he lacked other illustrations of his
theory.

'Mr Ferrier is a very good man,' said
Gwendoline, drawing figures upon the
gravel with the point of her parasol, 'and
doubtless he does good.   How hard it
seems that such a misfortune as you were
hinting at the other day should be im-
pending over him! I suppose there is no
doubt of the fact?'

'Unhappily, none whatever,' replied
the physician with a deep sigh.

'I almost wish you had never told me
about it,' said Gwendoline. 'It was terrible to hear that sweet little woman talk
but yesterday of going to Italy as soon as
she had got over her trouble, and I all the
time knowing that she was doomed never

to see her native land again—but instead of its bright landscapes and sunlit sea, to go down into the cold dark grave.'

'Yes, poor soul; yet that will certainly happen; and it is likely enough the new-born babe will share her fate. That is scarcely to be regretted, if (as is almost certain) the seeds of its mother's disease should lie within it. And, indeed, so terrible a family foe is consumption—the complaint, of all others, which seems to have a vendetta against an entire race—that Mr Ferrier will be fortunate if even his little Marion is spared to him.'

'The dear little thing seems very delicate,' said Gwendoline pitifully.

'Yes, a beautiful hot-house flower, like her mother,' assented the doctor; 'as fair, and almost as fragile. The whole prospect is so gloomy that I scarcely dare to exhibit it to the husband and father, and yet, sooner or later, it must be done.'

'That will be very dangerous, doctor,

surely? I should have thought it would
have killed poor Giulia at once to tell her
that she was like to die.'

'No doubt it would, and therefore she
must not be told. But I ought not much
longer to conceal the matter from her husband.'

'Well, that is one of those uncharacter-
istic statements with which you now and
then surprise me, my dear doctor, more
than I can say. Is it possible that you,
who are so wise, and who know men
so well, imagine that Mr Ferrier is a man
capable of hiding such a secret from one
he loves? Of course you will do your
duty—perform the etiquette which, I suppose, the Faculty imposes on you in such
cases—but such a course, I must say, ap-
pears to me to be the extremity of folly.
You magnify your calling, doctor, and perhaps, as compared with others, with reason; but certainly, in some matters, your

profession is as conventional as that of any fashionable preacher.'

'How so?' inquired the doctor, with an air half-serious and half-amused.

'Well, take the case in question. Nothing can save this poor woman, you tell me; though, to look at her, so bright and beautiful, the thing seems incredible to me —the story of her doom a mere nightmare; and yet, besides the risk of hastening the calamity, you must needs make this old man wretched before his time.'

'There is something of reason, Gwendoline, in what you say,' returned the physician thoughtfully; 'as indeed there always is, and it is doubtless worth consideration.—But was not that a ring at the front-door just now? You must be prepared for visits of congratulation this morning, of course.—Why, surely that is some one I know at the drawing-room window?'

'Yes; it is Mr Ferrier,' said Gwendoline quietly. 'How strange we should just have been talking about him! And see, he has brought out poor Giulia with him!'

CHAPTER VI.

ON the broad gravel-walk that ran between the whole frontage of the mansion
and the garden, were now standing a
married pair, whom no one who saw them
for the first time could possibly have taken
for man and wife. The husband might
have been a contemporary of Dr Gisborne's;
but if his frame was stouter, his eyes were
less bright, and indeed had already something of the lack-lustre look of advanced
senility, while his thin hair and neatly
trimmed whiskers were white as snow.
He had a quiet and not unthoughtful face;

but a physiognomist would have predicated
weakness from the formation of the mouth,
notwithstanding its pleasant and even
genial smile. Upon his arm leaned a
young woman, so youthful indeed as to be
almost like a child, notwithstanding that
she had already a little girl of her own of
three years old, and that she was soon
again to become a mother. She was very
beautiful; and it did not need the heavy
mantle which she wore, even on that mild
autumn morning, to show that she had been
accustomed to a far more genial climate
even than that of Cornwall. Her olive
skin and raven hair might have belonged
to a gipsy; but Giulia Ferrier had none of
the strength and hardihood of that wander-
ing tribe. Her cheeks had a colour more
brilliant, yet more limited in its extent,
than health ever bestows, and her large
black eyes had a preternatural lustre. She
was accustomed, in her half-playful, half-
complaining way, to speak of herself as

'the exotic;' and an exotic she was—a
flower of a genial clime transplanted to a
too hardy soil, a too vigorous air. Nor
was it only the climate to which she was
unsuited. English manners, English cus-
toms, English tastes, were more than alien
to her —they were antagonistic. The
well-meant civilities of 'the county,' which
had been freely extended to her, appeared
at best but clumsy courtesies. Its hospitalities were also oppressive; and on the
other hand, the most estimable families
beginning with Tre, Pol, and Pen were
quite unable to 'make Mrs Ferrier out.'
She adored her child, she had a passionate
love for flowers (the only natural taste in
which she could now indulge), and she had
the utmost respect for her husband. A
warmer feeling could scarcely be expected
from a girl of twenty towards one who
might have been her grandfather.

Their marriage had taken place under
circumstances that were somewhat roman-

tic, considering the character of the bridegroom. It was certainly curious that a
Scotch gentleman of mature age and Presbyterian convictions, who had passed all
his life in mercantile pursuits, should offer
his hand (with an income of many thou-
sands a year in it) to a penniless foreigner
of the Catholic faith; but this had actually
taken place. Her father, a struggling
painter, had died in Rome while Mr
Ferrier happened to be staying in the
Eternal City. She had been left forlorn
and friendless; and his kind heart had
taken pity upon her. He could not (thus
he reasoned with himself) leave her there
alone and unprotected, and only the more
likely, if she were well dowered, to be the
prey of some designing adventurer. But,
in fact, there was no necessity in the case
of one so beautiful as Giulia for even an
elderly gentleman to excuse himself at all.
They married, and, upon the whole, they
had lived very happily together; only the

poor girl had been always haunted with the desire of revisiting her native land, and she had at last coaxed from Mr Ferrier a reluctant permission to do so, so soon as the expected babe should be born, and the mother have gained sufficient strength for the journey. From the moment that his assent had been obtained, she had seemed a new creature, full of innocent mirth and joyful expectation—like a child who has been promised a new toy. It was only those two who were now advancing to meet herself and her husband across the garden who had the least suspicion that that promise could never be fulfilled.

Gwendoline, whose grace and beauty delighted Giulia's artistic eye, had always, of all their Cornish neighbours, been her favourite, and the greeting between the two girls was very cordial.

'You great courageous creature!' cried the latter in her pretty broken English (of which, however, she was not a little proud, as well as of her scraps of knowledge of our barbarian usages and phrases generally), and holding her friend at the extremity of her own slight arms, as if to get a complete view of such a heroine. 'How sleek and unruffled you look, after all your exploits.—Look at her, Bruce, dear! Is she not a wonder?'

'Miss Treherne has always struck me as being equal to any occasion that might require courage and self-command,' observed Mr Ferrier with polite elaboration.

'But it *must* have shaken you, my dear,' went on Giulia impetuously. 'It is impossible that even your nerves can have gone through such an ordeal as Fanny has just been describing to us without having suffered for it in some way. As for me, the very hint of a horrid brigand being so much as in the house would have killed me outright.'

'But they were not brigands, I assure you, my dear Giulia,' replied Gwendoline smiling. 'Not at all the picturesque sort of ruffians that are grown under your native skies, with peaked hats, and tasseled gaiters, and gracefully arranged shawls. They were in rags and tatters; and instead of a beautiful inlaid stiletto, each had a vulgar bludgeon. The whole affair was thoroughly English, and would have had no interest for an artist like you at all.'

'No interest? I never was so interested in anything in all my life. Pray, tell me all about it.—They had masks of crape, had they not? and an iron ring round their ankles; and one of them—yes, that is why you wear that handkerchief—pricked your lovely throat with the point of his wicked knife?'

'Why, you never mentioned that, Gwendoline,' said Dr Gisborne reprovingly.

'No, of course she didn't,' continued Giulia: 'she would die rather than confess herself to have been either frightened or hurt. But it is certain she must have been both; and what Bruce and I mean to do is to carry her back to Glen Druid this very day, to stay there, for change of air and scene, till she is recovered. If she will not come of her own free will, you must give us a certificate of the necessity of her removal, doctor, and then we will take her by force, for that is English law; besides, we have found out—like the brigands—that Sir Guy and his man are away, so that there is nobody to resist.—Come, I call upon you gentlemen, in the Queen's name—for that is the law too—to attach the person of Miss Gwendoline Treherne, and help me to put her in prison at Glen Druid.'

It was pitiful to hear her musical and childish talk—pitiful to watch her lively and graceful movements, as she laid her little hand in mimic arrest upon Gwendoline's rounded arm; and to know that all that vitality and beauty were doomed to perish, and she so totally unconscious of it. It was almost as pitiful to see the old man's delight and pride in his young wife's winning ways; and well might Dr Gisborne shrink from the task of telling him that there must soon remain of them nothing except a bitter memory.

'But you will come, Gwendoline?' urged Giulia with plaintive persuasion. 'It will be so much better for you than remaining here, where every breath of wind must sound like robbers; and you will be quite safe at Glen Druid, because there are five great hulking men in the house, and I don't know how many more about the grounds.'

'She is actually boasting of the extent of her establishment!' exclaimed Gwendoline smiling. 'My dear Giulia, how thoroughly acclimatized you are getting.'

'Nay, Miss Treherne,' interposed matter-of-fact Mr Ferrier gravely; 'I am sure

it was not my wife's intention to boast of
anything of the sort.'

'*I* boast?' cried Giulia in her turn.
'O dear, how dare anybody say that! I
wish we had no servants at all; I wish—'
She stopped suddenly, catching sight of a
distressed look upon her husband's face.
'I wish I was not such a naughty child,
dear Bruce,' said she with pathetic self-
reproach; and she put up her olive cheek,
tinged with a rose-blush, for the kind old
man to kiss.

'Well, for my part,' said Gwendoline
simply, 'I should like to change house-
holds with you, my dear. You should
have Adolphe at Glen Druid, and welcome; and all your people should come
and live in this great empty barrack,
where there would be plenty of room for
them, if nothing else. Then I should be
properly waited upon, do nothing for myself, and become the fine lady I should
like to be.'

'You dear, lazy darling, then come to Glen Druid!' cried Giulia rapturously. 'You shall never put foot to ground there, unless you please. We will sit in the greenhouse and gather fruit with the grape-catcher, without moving from our easy-chairs. You shall have my own maid, Susan, all to yourself, because she understands lazy people; and a horse—no, you shall not have a horse to yourself, because you would be running away from me; but we will have the pony-carriage all to ourselves, and you shall drive the little wretches, for you will not be afraid of them, as I am. O dear, how nice it will all be!'

'It will certainly be very nice,' said Gwendoline thoughtfully; 'at least very nice for *me*. But—'

'But, you would doubtless say, "I should not like to leave my father,"' observed Mr Ferrier kindly. 'Our invitation, however, of course extends to Sir

Guy also, if he will give us the pleasure of his company—though I know he loves his own roof when he is not in town.'

Giulia was silent, for she disliked Sir Guy above all men. His artificiality, which, in its would-be grace and pretended candour, seemed to ape her own naturalness, and to mock at it, was hateful to her. She thought him a selfish old wretch, who treated his daughter abominably; and his taking his valet with him, and leaving her without male protection the previous night, had been one of the topics of her discourse with her husband on their way to the Court that very morning. Gwendoline had never thought of her father's accompanying her. Her 'But' had had no reference to him whatever; she had looked towards Mr Ferrier, and affected to hesitate, in the hope that he would have finished her sentence for her in another manner, by joining his own entreaties, that she should return to Glen Druid, to

those of Giulia. She would not have had
Sir Guy under that roof with her just now,
for the most cogent reasons.

The situation might have been somewhat embarrassing but for the opportune
interposition of Dr Gisborne.

'I think I can answer for Sir Guy,'
said he, 'for it was only a day or two ago
that he was asking whether I did not
think a few weeks in London would not
be a beneficial change for him. When
a patient puts his case in that way, his
doctor always understands how to treat it,
and I told him he ought to go ; so that
little difficulty is easily settled.—As for
you, Miss Gwendoline' (and he gave her a
significant glance, which she well understood to refer to Mrs Ferrier), 'it is certainly my opinion that you ought to accept
this invitation.'

'Excellent man !' cried Giulia, clap-
ping her small hands. 'I never liked a
horrid doctor before.—Well, you know I

can't bear them, Bruce, with their long faces and their solemn head-shakings, which seem to foretell all sorts of horrors. They frighten me almost to death before they begin to cure me. — I don't mean to be rude to *you*, Dr Gisborne; so please to forgive me, if I seem to be so.'

'I quite forgive you, dear Mrs Ferrier,' said the physician with a smile that was a sad one, in spite of himself; 'and I trust it may be long before you have any cause to see me show a long face, or shake my head. It is most wise as well as kind of you to suggest this change for Gwendoline; and my certificate she shall have, if she cannot be induced to go with you without force of arms.'

'There, you hear!' cried Giulia joyfully. 'Now make your arrangements at once, my darling. Tell Fanny to pack your things, and of course we will take her with us in the carriage; for my husband is not too proud—are you, dear Bruce ?—to sit on the same seat with a waiting-maid.'

'Certainly not, my dear; I have nothing to be proud of,' returned Mr Ferrier in a tone that rather belied his words.

'Nay, nay; you offered me your own Susan, remember,' cried Gwendoline playfully, 'and I shall keep you to your word, Giulia. Glen Druid would not be the complete change which is to do me so much good if I took Fanny with me.' Next to her father, in fact, her waiting-maid would have been the most objectionable person to take with her, and the one even more likely—from her unquenchable loquacity—to injure her plans.

'Come just as you will, alone or attended, my dear Miss Treherne,' said Mr Ferrier (not perhaps without a feeling of gratitude for her having preserved him from having Fanny for his fellow-traveller), 'so long as you do come; and for my wife's sake.'

'What a *gauche* old man is this!'

thought Gwendoline. 'How difficult it will be to deal with him!'

'I trust we may be able to make Glen Druid sufficiently attractive to keep you with us for some time.'

'It is most kind of you to say so, Mr Ferrier. I will do my best to repay you by being of as much use as I can to your treasure here, and to my favourite little playmate, Marion.—Now, do you sit down here, dear Giulia, for I am sure you must be tired of standing—' and she wheeled towards her a garden-chair—'while I run in to tell Fanny to pack up.'

'I am not at all tired, darling,' replied Mrs Ferrier; but as her friend moved away, she sat down wearily enough, nevertheless.

'What a kind, dear creature Gwendoline is, and so unaffected—is she not, doctor?—but there, I need not ask, for I know you have been in love with her for years.'

'That is true, my dear madam,' said

the physician, smiling gravely: 'I must own the soft impeachment. Nothing but the disparity,' he was about to say, 'in our ages—' but recollecting on the instant in whose presence he stood, he turned the sentence as swiftly and naturally as swallow on the wing—'the disparity of birth has prevented me from declaring myself her devoted lover. I am quite a *novus homo*, and the Trehernes were at Bedivere, as folks say, in the days of the Cornish giants.'

'Good blood is nevertheless a good thing,' observed the possessor of Glen Druid, with a more decided northern accent than was usual with him; 'and so far as birth goes—though some of them have but little siller—the Ferriers of Lanarkshire can count a direct progenitor for every finger.'

'Does that include the thumbs, sir?' inquired the physician, with an air of much interest.

'It does, sir,' said the old man, drawing himself to his full height. 'I am the tenth male of my line; and, please God, if all things go well—' and he cast a significant glance at the unconscious Giulia, to whom pedigree was a dead-letter—'there may be an eleventh, come Christmas next, or thereabouts, as I am given to understand.'

'Amen!' said Dr Gisborne with tender gaiety. 'Let us hope it may be so!'

CHAPTER VII.

GLEN DRUID.

GLEN DRUID, despite its antiquated name, was quite a modern mansion, purchased of him who built it by Mr Ferrier, and transformed by the latter from a merely handsome country-seat into one of the most beautiful and perfect residences in the south of England. Since Giulia had always so regretted her native land, her husband, himself greatly averse to return thither, had gallantly resolved to bring Italy as much as possible into Cornwall. The climate, although moist, was really warm, and every flower and plant to which she had been accustomed was either made to grow in the sheltered gardens, or in the vast conservatory upon which the great drawing-room opened. In the house itself, again, were flowers in profusion; and flowering-trees alternated in the fine hall and corridor with exquisite statuary. Pictures of the old masters adorned every sitting-room; but Giulia's boudoir was hung round with the works of her own father's brush, with each of which was associated in her mind some story, which was now a tender recollection.

In curious contrast with the luxury within the house, and with the artificial beauty of its grounds and gardens, was the natural scenery which surrounded the place, and made it seem an oasis as well as a paradise. It stood in a little bay on the western coast; north and south of it stretched a long line of granite cliffs; on the east—from the winds of which it was, however, well shielded—lay a vast waste

of moorland, once, say the learned, posi-
tively, a forest, but now without a stick of
timber. There was nothing, indeed, that
stood higher than its patches of gorse, for
miles, except a stone erection, the nature of
which might possibly have puzzled you,
but about which the learned were equally
sure. It consisted of three mighty stones,
with a fourth upon the top of them, of such
a size that how it could ever have been
hoisted to its position in pre-scientific days
was a marvel in itself. These few materials formed quite a stately dwelling; and
so far as the roof was concerned, they
might have served as such (without any
calling on the landlord for repairs, although
your lease had been one of those lengthy
ones extending to nine hundred and ninety-
nine years); but the sides were undeniably
draughty for such a purpose. The natives,
as usual, attributed its construction to the
Cornish giants, one of whom, it was suggested, had left his three-legged stool in

that exposed situation ; but our antiqua-
rian friends termed it a cromlech or ancient
burying-place.   Beneath it was doubtless
interred some hardy chief, who had expressed a wish, since the north-easters had
seemed to do him good during his lifetime, to be buried where he could always
hear them blow.

But wild and bare as was the landscape
behind Glen Druid, it was tame compared
with the coast-scenery upon which it
looked down.   There, walls of rock op-
posèd themselves in storm to the whole
power of the Atlantic, and at all times
bore fearful traces of the conflict.   On a
quiet summer day, indeed to see them
standing out of the blue waveless sea, so
seamed, and rugged, and defiant, gave
them even a more striking appearance than
in storm ; they looked like frowning veter-
ans, who, in some truce-time, which may
at any moment be broken by a smiling
but treacherous foe, stand sternly to their

arms, showing their dints and scars in justification of their grim mistrust.

On the south, the curve of the bay was formed by a huge promontory—the advance-guard of all the rocks upon that coast, and called locally, from some fancied resemblance of shape, the Warrior's Helm. But vaster far even than that famous headgear which so inconvenienced the Lord of Otranto, it was only at a great distance that you could catch the likeness which had won for it its name. To one who stood in the terraced gardens of Glen Druid, it was merely a picturesque black crag, around which, and up even to whose beetling summit, a pathway had with infinite pains been excavated, which also descended to the sands of what was called Horseshoe Bay. A certain barren grandeur at all times, then, distinguished the seaward view from the mansion : but when the elemental strife was raging, it was grand indeed : then the great arching billows rushed in with angry moan, and gave the Warrior's Helm a creamy crest; and raged and roared among the stubborn rocks, and gained a vantage ground, to lose it the next instant in such a whirl of fight around some pinnacle as might take place about the body of a monarch slain in battle; and in the conflict as to who shall keep him—friend or foe—the corpse itself is torn, and one retires with half the ghastly trophy, and one stands its ground.   At times, too, luckless ships were driven in ; and, as though they belonged to sea, and not to land, the inhospitable granite sentinels denied them haven, and calmly listened to their signal-guns for help, and calmly watched them dash themselves to pieces far below.   And yet, within a few yards of all this wild remorseless grandeur, lay the wall-gardens and pineries of Glen Druid, teeming with fruit and flower.

'How charmingly beautiful is all about this splendid home of yours!' exclaimed

Gwendoline to her friend and hostess, as, followed at a respectful distance by the latter's waiting-maid, Susan Ramsay, they moved slowly up and down a lower terrace which gave access to the Warrior's Helm. 'It seems to me so strange that you should wish to exchange it for any other.'

'Ah, but you don't know Italy, my Italy,' answered Giulia enthusiastically. 'I would rather live in Italy on the sum that Susan yonder is paid for her yearly wage — which would indeed be almost riches there—than with all the luxury that surrounds me at Glen Druid.'

'That is incomprehensible to me, my dear,' said Gwendoline, looking at her friend with something more than curiosity. 'Now, for my part, if I were in your place, and judging from what I have seen during the few days that I have been your guest, I should have nothing to desire. Dr Gisborne is the only person I have ever known to express opinions like your own, and yet you and he are so different. Sometimes I think you are both hypocrites, and do not really feel that contempt for wealth and luxury which you express ; and sometimes, on the other hand, I think myself dreadfully worldly, in comparison with such virtuous folks—for I do frankly own I love both power and splendour.'

'And you ought to have them, dear Gwendoline,' replied her companion simply : 'that brow of yours was made for an earl's coronet at the very least—that is what everybody says. And yet to see you so gentle and unaffected, bearing with all my foolish whims, and taking to my darling Marion as though you were her nurse ! Even Mr Ferrier, who is not observant of such things in general, noticed the—what do you call it now ?—the—'

'The incongruity, I suppose you mean,' said Gwendoline, smiling with very genuine pleasure, not for the compliment's sake, but from the secret reflection : 'Then the old man has noticed my care for his wife and child already.'—'But, in truth, dear Giulia, there is no anomaly in the affair at all. I might, for that matter, be only practising for my future livelihood; for if anything were to happen to Sir Guy, I must needs become a humble companion, if not a nursemaid, or else starve.'

'Starve!' ejaculated Giulia with a little shudder. 'What dreadful words you use, Gwendoline. The idea, to begin with, of your ever wanting a home while Glen Druid here stands where it is! But I know what English ladies mean by starving and being left without a shilling: they mean, instead of driving two pretty little ponies, they can only afford to keep one. Now *I*, Gwendoline, have been really poor. When dear papa died, I was left with nothing, absolutely nothing, except a few what you call sterling pounds, and even they were bespoken for just debts.'

'I do, however, assure you, Giulia,

upon my honour,' returned the other earnestly, 'that when Sir Guy dies, my own case will resemble what you describe as having been yours.'

'But my papa always *looked* as though he had no money,' exclaimed the wondering Giulia, 'although, dear soul, he was always gay and cheerful, and we dwelt in a poor house. But you, who live in a castle, and whose father is a man of rank —Sir Guy spends much upon himself, I know, but is it possible he has spent *all*?'

Gwendoline cast down her eyes in silence. She desired that the pity which was filling Giulia's tender heart should take its full course. 'Let us talk of something more cheerful, dear,' said she abruptly. 'How blue the sea is this morning, and how exquisitely it contrasts with the white sands! I suppose it would fatigue you too much to venture down?'

Poor Giulia was not perhaps without some secret misgiving respecting the fra-

gile tenure upon which she held her life;
at all events, as is usual in such cases, she
resented any suggestion of her being
weakly and delicate, and was obstinate to
prove herself otherwise. 'Fatigued! Why
should I be fatigued? I should like a
walk upon the sparkling sands above all
things;' and she moved briskly towards
the winding path.

But instantly there was a sound of
hurrying footsteps, and Susan Ramsay was
at the side of her young mistress. 'You
must not go down yonder, madam—indeed, you must not, said she firmly. It
looks easy enough to descend, but the
way back again is very steep.'

'You are quite right, Susan,' said
Gwendoline approvingly; 'I was just
saying that it would be much too fa-
tiguing.'

'O yes, I know I am right, miss,' replied Susan, coldly.—'You know, dear
mistress,' added she with earnestness, 'how

particular Dr Gisborne is about your not
exerting yourself too much.'

'I am not Dr Gisborne's slave, nor
yours either, Susan, though you seem to
think sometimes that it is you who are the
mistress, and I your servant,' exclaimed
Giulia petulantly. 'I shall certainly have
a run on the sands; and I will thank you
to go to the house and fetch Miss Marion—
there is nothing she likes so much as pick-
ing up shells.'

Susan cast one hasty glance at Gwendoline, as though to ask her to add her
entreaties to her own; but perhaps she
read in her face that she would only receive a lukewarm assistance. At all events,
she turned away the next instant, without
a word, to execute her mistress's orders.

'Susan is an excellent creature, but she
takes too much upon herself,' exclaimed
Mrs Ferrier. 'I am really half afraid of
her, she has so strong a will.'

'Scotch people often have,' remarked

Gwendoline; 'but I am sure she is fond of you in her way, and only wants a little tact. Let me take your arm down this steep place, my dear, so that we may steady one another.'

And so they descended into Horseshoe Bay, Gwendoline, under pretence of the copartnership, almost entirely support-ing Giulia, whose trembling limbs were very ill qualified for the task imposed upon them. On the level sand, however, she tripped along gaily enough; and when her child was brought to her, it was not easy to say which of the two enjoyed themselves more artlessly among the shells and weeds. The parallel was the completer, since, when she ventured too near the waves, and incurred the risk of a wetting, she was reproved by Susan as Marion was, as though she also had been a child.

'Why, what is this?' cried Giulia pre-sently. 'Is it possible the good folks of Saint Medards have been having a feast here, and forgot to drink their wine? See, here is a bottle, and with the cork in it undrawn.'

'Yes,' said Gwendoline; 'but there is nothing inside it, if I know my compatriots.'

'Ah, but there is, I tell you—there is something white: it looks like a letter.'

'Then it is a message from the Sea,' exclaimed Gwendoline with interest. 'Some folks on shipboard, I mean, have written the story of their peril, and confided it to the waves. That is quite common. Have you not seen such things in the bay before?'

'Never, never,' said Giulia sadly, 'though I have often heard of them. Poor souls!'

'But why not break the bottle?'

'I dare not. Do *you* do it, Gwendoline. I do hate anything dreadful. I must hear it, however, now I have seen it. What does the writing say?'

Gwendoline unfolded a rough slip of paper, which the salt water had not touched, and read as follows, while the two women with beating hearts, and little Marion with wondering eyes, clustered about her. NORTH SEA, *April* 3 ('That is nearly five months ago, you see, dear; so their sufferings, whatever they were, have long been over')—*On board the Constance from Gefle.* ('Where is Gefle, I wonder? I never so much as heard of the place.')

'Never mind that,' exclaimed Giulia anxiously. 'Do, pray, go on. Poor souls, poor souls!'

In distress, being near to sink, as the brig has sprung a leak two days ago, and the water always increasing, notwithstanding all our attempts to prevent it, we have now come very near the last moment of our lives.

'O Lord, have mercy upon them, and forgive them their sins!' exclaimed Susan piously.

Wherefore, although we must never see our

*native land again, we beg him or her who may
find this letter to inform the public of our misfortune.*

'Poor creatures! We must send a
copy of this to the *Times* to-morrow.—My
darling Giulia, what is the matter?' Mrs
Ferrier had turned suddenly quite white,
and, but for Susan's aid, would have fallen
upon the sands.

'We must never see our native land
again,' moaned she. 'Oh, how I pity
them!'

'But, dear heart, only consider they
have been in heaven, let us hope, this long
time,' urged Susan, 'which is better than
any earthly abiding-place.'

But her young mistress only shook her
head, and covered her eyes with her
hands.

'Marion, darling,' whispered Gwendoline, 'put your arms round mamma's neck,
and kiss her.'

The little child, perceiving her mother's

grief, though without in the least understanding its cause, obeyed readily enough;
and her embrace, as Gwendoline had
shrewdly guessed, proved the best cordial
that could have been administered. It
was not only pity for others which was
affecting poor Mrs Ferrier thus, but also
apprehensions 'for herself; and the kisses
of her child diverted her. thoughts into
another channel.

'My sweet Marion, we will go together
to Italy,' said she, caressing her, 'and
both get well and strong. The sun is
always shining there, and the great hills
stand out against the blue sky.'

'And the gapes,' said Marion, who had
an eye, common to her time of life, for the
material productions of nature, rather than
for its picturesque beauties—'the gapes
you said gow in the open air, and me can
reach 'em my own self without the long
tatcher.'

Gwendoline laughed heartily at this.

'Come home and get the grape-catcher at
once, Marion, for I am sure you deserve a
bunch. Susan will carry you up the hill,
and mamma and I will follow.' In which
order the party accordingly returned; Mrs
Ferrier being so exhausted by the time
she reached the top that she had to retire
to her room for the rest of the day; and
her husband and Gwendoline dined alone
together in stately fashion. The grandeur
of the entertainment suited her better than
the company; though she flattered herself
that the rigid courtesy of Mr Ferrier
towards her was melting a little.

'It is impossible, however,' reflected
she as she lay awake that night, as her
custom was, and reviewed the day's proceedings, 'that Giulia can have any real
affection for him; and as for this passionate desire to revisit Italy, I think I know
the secret of it. I am much mistaken if,
when she came to England as Mr Ferrier's
bride, she did not leave a lover in Italy.

If so, I am sorry for her, for it is certain she will never see him, poor fragile little woman. I began to fear I should scarcely have dragged her up that cliff alive!'

CHAPTER VIII.

SUSAN RAMSAY'S VIEW OF AFFAIRS.

THERE are a good many mischievous creeds which are believed in by society at large as though they were true faith; and, on the other hand, there are a few popular errors which it would be better for the world had they more foundation in fact. Of the latter, the following are examples: that your true aristocrat is rarely insolent; that a bully is *always* a coward; and that children are never deceived by a mere pretence of fondness for them. This last was proved utterly untrue in the case of Marion and Gwendoline. Gwendoline was not

fond of Marion, her character being one of
those exceptional ones among young women
to which child-nature is not attractive;
but she laid herself out to please her young
friend, and she succeeded. She was never
so occupied but that she could put aside
book, pen, or needle, to have a romp with
the child. She was always ready for a
run with her in the garden, or a scramble
upon the Warrior's Helm, taking matronly
care to hold fast that trusting little hand
wherever the path was perilous. On wet
days she would take her on her knee, and
show her pictures or tell her fairy stories
by the hour. By these means, she not only
reaped her reward in a plentiful crop of
affection from her small playmate, but won
golden opinions from her parents.

Mr Ferrier would often express his
fears, in his grave way, that the child was
trespassing upon Miss Treherne's good nature, though he received her assurance
that 'she doted upon children, and espe-

cially upon good ones, like Marion,' with the most perfect faith; while his wife only lamented that she was not strong enough to play her friend's part in these romps and gambols, which were in reality gradually transferring the love of her own little one from herself to Gwendoline. She had not the least suspicion or jealousy of the guest who made herself so useful to her in a hundred ways, and not in one officiously. She felt better for her presence in body and mind; for not only did Gwendoline, without the least parade of assistance, save her from physical fatigue, but kept her cheerful by her lively and graceful companionship, and by high spirits that never seemed to flag. Without sentiment, save her passionate love for absent Piers, and without sympathy, Gwendoline had a marvellous adaptability, which stood her in good stead for both. Her tact in pleasing was so consummate that it fell little short of geniality, and might have been easily taken for it by more incredulous eyes than those of simple Giulia.   Her fine voice, when she sang to her hostess—her brilliant execution, when she played—seemed to lack no feeling ; it was supplied by the listener's own spiritual nature.   She read aloud to her the poets of her land, and the 'soft bastard Latin,' syllabled by one so divinely .fair, seemed to take the exile's soul with a new bliss.   In short, Giulia yielded herself up a willing victim to these pleasant arts, and grew to love and to lean upon her friend with a feverish fondness that was in itself disease.   And all this time Death was beckoning to her with his silent finger, and drawing nearer and nearer to her every day.

Mr Ferrier knew, of course, that his wife was delicate, but attributed her later and later rising of a morning, her earlier withdrawal to her couch at night, to her condition, and to the winter season (always trying to the fragile woman), which had now set in with rigour. There was only one person in the Glen Druid household who suspected the true state of affairs, and who even suspected the guest. Gwendoline, whose magical beauty fascinated the very footmen, and whose gracious affability disarmed the envy of the domestics of her own sex, had failed to make a favourable impression upon Susan Ramsay. Perhaps, although the mother had forgiven Gwendoline for engrossing the affections of the child, the nurse had not— for Susan was Marion's head-nurse, as well as Mrs Ferrier's maid; or perhaps Gwendoline's very charms and accomplishments had placed the puritanical Scotchwoman in antagonism to her. But, at all events, Susan had never been fascinated with her, for it was not her way to be fascinated, like the other members of the household; and the more she watched her—and she watched her very closely—the less she liked her mistress's new friend. She held her tongue, as it was her nature to do, but she thought a good deal about Miss Treherne and her ways, and more and more unfavourably. She even gave herself the trouble to reflect upon her antecedents, of which she knew something, from Gwendoline's own maid, and would have liked to know more. But Fanny had been dismissed rather summarily from Bedivere Court within a week of her young lady's departure from it. The excuse was ready at hand, in the indiscretion with which she carried on her flirtations with Monsieur Adolphe; but the real cause lay in the waiting-maid's too garrulous tongue. Even as it was, this had done Gwendoline an ill turn, for it had informed Susan that at one time at least the belle of the county had had a lover; and was it not very strange, and even suspicious, that in that young lady's many confidential chats with Mrs Ferrier, to which the waiting-maid was often a privileged listener, she should never have descanted upon that attractive theme? Reticent enough upon other subjects, even Susan liked to talk about Sam Barland, the apothecary's head-assistant at St Medards, to whom she had been engaged for years, and might marry to-morrow, but for certain far-sighted and prudential reasons of her own; and it was not natural, she held, in Gentle or Simple, to have been courted by a laddie, and not crack about it to one's friends.

Miss Gwendoline, then, was, in her eyes, 'a deep one,' to begin with; and in the next place, she was a wicked one, for she never went to kirk. It was just excus-able, thought Susan, in the case of her own mistress, brought up among outlandish folk, in the faith of the Scarlet Woman, that she should not take advantage of the spiritual comforts which Mr Ferrier had furnished for the locality, in the shape of a Presbyterian church and preacher; but that Miss Treherne should pass the Sabbath at Glen Druid very much as though it were a week-day, and decline to attend church at St Medards, under the transparent pretext of keeping her friend and hostess company, was little better than rank heathenism. If Mrs Ferrier was so ill as to need folks to stay with her when they ought to be at public worship, it was high time that the puir blinded creature, who thought so little of her soul, should be made aware of her condition.

Susan had learned from Mr Samuel Barland that the medicines prescribed for her mistress by Dr Gisborne were not of a nature to restore health, but only to give relief; and the spiritual condition of her mistress, as we have hinted, gave conscientious Susan as much anxiety as her bodily ailment. And yet she might be wrong about the latter point—it seemed so strange that Dr Gisborne should keep silence on the matter, if there was real danger—and therefore she still hesitated to confide her suspicions to her master, of whose displeasure she stood in wholesome fear; still less could she venture to confide to him her doubts of Gwendoline, which indeed were at best but shadowy misgivings; and her good sense told her that to make an accusation without proof would be only to strengthen the hands that already wielded so much power beneath her master's roof.

An event had recently taken place, however, which bade fair to bring Susan's indignation up to the explosive point— namely, the arrival of Sir Guy Treherne at Glen Druid. In Susan's eyes, this elegant and gay old gentleman was the very embodiment of Satan; and his attendant, Monsieur Adolphe, a ministering fiend. They talked together, doubtless upon the most abominable subjects, in a language that was unknown to her. There was nothing in the house, in dining-room or servants' hall, which was too good for

either of them, or which both, in their
several ways, did not take as a matter of
course. The way in which the latter,
whose faith, as she had been assured, was
plighted to absent Fanny, 'went on'
with such of the female servants as were
young and pretty, was scandalous. If he
had dared to show any such marked attentions to herself, she would have very soon
let him know what she thought of them
and of him ; and yet she resented, incon-
sistently enough, that he treated with such
respectful coldness the *fiancée* (as he once
called her, to her great annoyance, for she
thought it was 'some impudence') of Mr
Samuel Barland, who, in truth, had achieved an age beyond which the female sex
failed to interest the fastidious Frenchman.
It annoyed her exceedingly to see the
deference with which this gentleman was
treated by the authorities of the servants'
hall, but still more so to observe the respect
in which Sir Guy was held by her master.

The butler had brought word how he was permitted to jeer at table against sacred things without reproof from staid Mr Ferrier; and indeed she herself had seen him shrug his shoulders on a Sunday, when he was asked if he was going to church, in a manner that made her long to whip him.

No wonder that Miss Gwendoline—although she made no allowance for her on that account—should be such a godless young person, with the bringing-up that she must have had from such a father. Susan's only comfort under the circumstances was to reflect, that Sir Guy was certainly going at no distant date to a place where his rank would not be considered, and his long ages of ancestry would be as nothing compared to the period for which he would be doomed to suffer torment. It might have been some mitigation to Susan's irritated feelings that her mistress seemed to dislike Sir Guy as much as *she* did, but that, in Mrs Ferrier's case, this objection to the baronet only made her cling more fondly to his daughter, whom she considered as his social victim. Susan, for her part, disposed of that sentimental circumstance by two courses of reasoning, none the less convincing to herself that they were incompatible with one another. In the first place, she argued that Miss Gwendoline was just the last person in the world to permit her interests to be sacrificed to those of any other human being; and secondly, that if they were so, she richly deserved it.

It was while matters at Glen Druid were in this very unsatisfactory condition, in Susan's view, with Gwendoline dominant, and Sir Guy an honoured, if not a respected, guest, that a circumstance occurred in connection with them, of so astounding and compromising a character, that the knowledge of it seemed to place both father and daughter in the waiting-maid's power.

It was Gwendoline's custom to rise early at Glen Druid, and to perform those duties of the breakfast-table to which her hostess would scarcely have been equal, even had it not been now her invariable custom to take that meal in her own room. Sir Guy elevated his eyebrows when he saw his stately daughter cutting Mr Ferrier's newspaper for him, and humouring his tastes in cream and sugar; but he would have raised them even higher had he known that when the two were alone it was not an unusual circumstance for their host to read out portions of his private letters to Gwendoline, and to await her comments, not to say receive her advice, with considerable deference. But on a certain morning it so happened that she was not punctually at her post—Giulia, who had passed a worse night than common, having detained her with fretful complaints—and, as ill luck would have it, there was a letter from Piers Mostyn waiting for

her beside her plate, and within range of
Sir Guy's observant eye.   She took it up
with the utmost coolness, and with a quiet
' Excuse me,' read it through without
moving a muscle; but her lover's indiscretion—for she had expressly enjoined on
him not to write until he had heard from
her—annoyed her exceedingly. Of course,
Mr Ferrier paid no attention to the circumstance : he would have made no remark,
nor have desired to make one, had she
received fifty letters by one post; but she
knew that it would presently provoke com-
ment from her father, whom she had informed that all relations between herself
and Piers were broken off; and might just
possibly—since the letters she had received
at Glen Druid had been hitherto from
ladies only—attract the notice of others.
Unlike her sex, Gwendoline never ran a
risk, however small, when it could possibly be avoided; and had she been on
the turf, would have hedged every shilling,

no matter how much of 'a moral' the
event she stood to win on might have
appeared. When the risk was incurred,
she never shut her eyes to the consequences, but made up her mind to meet
the worst. She did not know, of course,
that Susan Ramsay—as heedful of the
slightest indications afforded by an enemy
as herself—had noticed the superscription
on the envelope when she came to take her
mistress's breakfast up-stairs, but she was as
much prepared for such a misfortune as to
meet the more certain remonstrances of Sir
Guy. Gwendoline left nothing to chance;
perhaps she was not without some vague
idea that she was thus making herself independent of Providence itself.

The letter, which she presently took
out with her upon the lower terrace, and
re-read carefully again and again, walking
slowly to and fro, contained no great matter, but it affected her powerfully, nevertheless. As the blind are transported by

music, and the dumb by colour, so she, with whom so many of the spiritual senses were shut, was all the more given up to her passion for her lover; if she cared for no other human being in the world, she was devoted to handsome Piers Mostyn. His written words were dearer a thousand times than the presence of any other; and she almost forgave him now, in the rapturous delight she reaped from his very act of disobedience. And yet there was little in his letter, one would have thought, to have given an affianced woman pleasure. It was written from a great country-house in Yorkshire, at present filled with a large company of guests, and was mainly descriptive of his gaiety (though he was absent from her), and of his flirtations (though he had plighted to her his troth). But, at all events, he was open enough in what he said; if the tone of his epistle was frivolous throughout where it was not bitter, it was not the less characteristic on that account; and reading his words, she might easily imagine that he himself was beside her, with his light laugh and brilliant cynicism. Moreover, there was here and there a passionate protestation of affection for her, that made up for all shortcomings and misdoings, and which brought, as she read it, the colour to her cheek and the love-light to her eye. 'You need not fear, notwithstanding all this impatience, darling,' wrote he, after one of those fond paragraphs, 'that I shall not wait for you, for there is no opportunity for doing otherwise: all the lovely creatures that I have just described entirely understand that I am quite ineligible. Perhaps their mothers have told them so, but it is quite as likely that their own fine perceptions have informed them that I am a Detrimental. We flirt, of course, immensely; they practise upon me in that way as though I were a lay-figure; but though, to do them justice, they draw no very hard-and-fast line,

in that way, they make me quite understand it is only a flirtation and nothing
more; one of them actually asked me if it
was true that I had been in a marching-
regiment, and got so brown in India! So
you may imagine the social position that
had been assigned to me. When I told
her how I had been in the diplomatic line,
and got my tan from the Persian sun, I
did not improve matters. "Ah!" said
she, "an *un*paid *attaché*, I suppose;"
with such a stress upon the first sylla-
ble. So, you see, my beautiful darling—'
and Gwendoline murmured these words
aloud as a mother crows over her babe
—' I am yours, and ever yours, per-
force.'

'If you please, ma'am,' said a cold and
quiet voice, all the colder and calmer by
contrast with those burning words, 'Miss
Marion asked to be allowed to join you on
the terrace.'

Rapt in her own honeyed thoughts, she

had not observed Susan Ramsay's approach, who now stood beside her, holding little Marion's hand, and looking at her as though her small black eyes were bradawls. 'Dear little thing!' said Gwendoline, stooping down to pat the child, and at the same time to hide her own confusion; 'I am afraid I must disappoint you this morning, pretty one.' But here she caught Sir Guy's well-preserved figure bearing down upon her from the house; and reflecting within herself that the little girl would form a convenient third in the expected meeting, should it prove embarrassing, she added : 'But there, I can never resist my little pet. — You may leave her, Susan; and tell your mistress not to be nervous about her getting on the rocks, for that we shall not leave the garden.'

Now, Miss Marion had not asked to be allowed to join her 'booful Dwendoline,' as in her baby-talk she designated her new friend, until she had had that idea suggested to her by Susan herself, who wished to have a pretext for intruding on Miss Treherne's meditations; and now that she was dismissed, the waiting-maid did not return to the house, as Gwendoline took for granted she would do, but retired to an arbour in the upper terrace, from which, unseen, she could both see and hear much that was passing below. *She* also had marked Sir Guy's approach, and argued rightly that the indolent baronet, who seemed to prefer a rocking-chair by the fire to any outdoor exercise her master could offer to him, had not made that unaccustomed pilgrimage down so many stone steps, on that bright but frosty morning, without an object, which was probably a private talk with his daughter.

'Now, if I can only look over both their hands at once,' thought Susan, bor-

rowing a metaphor from a diversion she
had seen practised in the servants' hall,
and which had often excited her vehement
reprehension, 'then I shall know better
how to play my cards.'

CHAPTER IX.

SIR GUY AND GWENDOLINE.

NOTHING could be quieter or more de-
mure than Sir Guy's aspect as he walked
slowly, and with that slightly balancing air
which advanced age, in combination with
high-heeled boots, is apt to produce, towards his daughter and her little playmate.
Nothing less like an indignant father bent
upon strong measures with his disobedient
offspring could be imagined than that unruffled though not unwrinkled face, with a
sort of peach-bloom upon the cheeks, of
which himself and his man Adolphe alone
knew the secret. Partly as typifying the

careless gaiety of his disposition, and partly
because he was conscious that in that
trembling of his fingers lay his weak point,
it was his custom to keep at least one hand
in his pocket; the other, when abroad,
was generally provided with a clouded
cane, which steadied while it seemed to
adorn his movements. A closer observer
of human nature than she who was now
watching him in secret with all her eyes,
might have gathered from the unnecessary
force with which his cane was brought
down on the gravel at every step, that he
who carried it was not at ease in his mind;
but to Susan, the baronet looked the beau-
idéal of sleekness and prosperity, and her
mind flew instantly for comfort to the end
of the green bay tree, and of him who was
dressed in purple and fine linen every day.

To her intense chagrin, the baronet
addressed his daughter in that outlandish
tongue to which she had so often thanked
Heaven that she was a stranger, but which

she would for once have given one of her own sharp ears to comprehend.

'There is no occasion for so much prudence, papa,' was Gwendoline's reply in English. 'This is too small a pitcher to carry a long ear; and since I know that you are going to scold me, it is better to use the language that is made for scolding. Let us keep our French for enjoyment, I do beg.'

Gwendoline's face was calm and even smiling, and she playfully pushed little Marion's ball before her with her foot as she spoke, and bade the child run after it.

'You had a letter from Piers Mostyn this morning, Gwendoline?'

'Yes, papa. I have just been reading it.'

'And yet you told me that you had broken with him altogether, and forbidden him to correspond with you.'

'And so I did,' said she; 'but all people have not the talent for obedience that your daughter possesses. He has written to me, as you say ; and after all, there is no such great harm done.'

'You don't know that,' returned the baronet sharply. 'What I saw, others may have seen ; and he may write some day when there may be sharper eyes upon the look-out than there are at Glen Druid. It is greatly against a girl, in some men's view, that she should keep up a correspondence of this sort.'

'It takes two to make a correspondence, papa—as it does a quarrel.' She spoke the last words with great deliberation, and confronted her father face to face. 'I have never written to Piers, and I do not intend to write to him. I told him that I should not do so, and I always keep my word.'

'Then it's a piece of impertinence on Mr Mostyn's part to pester you in this manner, and I shall let him know that that is my opinion. Whom is the fellow sponging upon ? for I noticed that the letter had a Yorkshire postmark, and his brother's place is not in Yorkshire.'

'He is staying with his cousin, Lord Carruthers, at Stonegate, and has been there for a week or so; just as we are staying here with the Ferriers, who are not our cousins.'

'Pooh, pooh! there is no parallel in the two cases at all, and you know that as well as I do. This Piers Mostyn has not a roof to his head, nor a shilling that he can call his own to buy him a night's lodging. He can be only welcome at Stonegate to take the bores off his lordship's hands, or to turn over the leaves of his young wife's music-book.'

'Well, I would not write to him to tell him that, if I were you—nor anything else. You can quite safely leave him to me, papa. When you last spoke to me upon this matter, your unreserve and frankness were so complete that it was quite impossible to misunderstand you. I am sensible of the state of my own affairs; and I dare say almost as much interested in them as you are yourself.'

'This letter did not look as if such was the case, Gwendoline; that's all I meant to say,' remarked Sir Guy in mollified tones. 'You're a very clever girl, I know; but all women are fools when a young fellow like Mostyn pretends to be in love with them. I don't deny the vagabond has good gifts—far from it. If he had ten thousand a year, and would pass his word to give up whist, you should marry him to-morrow. But without wishing to hurt your feelings, my dear, and allowing him to have good taste in his *tendresse* for yourself, Gwendoline, Piers is a born fool. I have watched his play at *the Portarlington*, and no man, no matter what his fortune or his luck, could stand his ground for long with such ideas as he has. A man who finesses with king, ten— But, there! you know nothing of what I'm talking about.

What I want you to understand is this: that time is money with a girl in your position more than in anything, and that here at Glen Druid (I wish you would send that confounded child away) you are losing your time.'

'Not altogether, papa, I think,' said Gwendoline quietly.—'The ball is at my feet; and see, my darling Marion, I am going to send it for you farther than ever;' and off toddled the small creature, leaving her seniors to converse alone together as before.

'Well, not altogether, I grant,' said Sir Guy gravely. 'It is always well to gain a foothold with people like the Ferriers. If the worst comes to the worst, you will always have a home here, I presume: you have made friends of the Mammon of Unrighteousness, and they can scarcely have a more pleasant habitation to offer one than Glen Druid.'

Susan Ramsay in her place of espial

lifted up hand and eye aghast at this idea ; to hear her excellent master spoken of in that manner, and this Satan in polished leather boots applying Scripture to his own ends !

'Yes, the Ferriers are stanch friends, papa, I assure you ; but I fancy you have found *that* out already for yourself.'

'Not at all, not at all, my dear,' answered Sir Guy with a wave of his cane. 'It is true I have had a little "business transaction" with our friend and host, in which he showed a liberal spirit. But he got his *quid pro quo*, good moorland, for his money : all between the sky and the central fire is his, my dear; and who knows but that there may be copper and tin beneath that unpromising-looking turf, enough to repay him ten times over.'

'I am glad it was quite a business transaction,' remarked Gwendoline coldly. 'I was afraid you might be laying yourself and me under some sense of obligation.'

'Not a bit, my dear Gwendoline,' said the baronet, striking his chest theatrically, which, being much padded, only emitted a dull thud: 'the obligation, if any, lies on the other side. There are few Scotchmen, and, for the matter of that, few English, I thank Heaven, but like to be on intimate terms with any one who has a handle to his name. Talk of the lever— there is no power in this charming country to be compared with that of the *handle;* if one only possess, in addition, a few ancestors (and you may dig bushels of yours and mine out of the Bedivere vaults), it is quite surprising how marketable the property comes to be.' And Sir Guy Treherne gave a patronizing smile upon sea and sky, as though they too might be not insensible of his affability, and rattled the sovereigns in his unaccustomed pocket. 'But after all, my dear Gwendoline,' resumed he gravely, 'the affair you hint at was a small thing; a mere retaining fee in respect of that in-

terest which I hope I shall never cease to
feel in your private affairs, and not to be
mentioned in the same breath with them.
Moreover, the moor is gone, and I have
nothing more to sell.   What I have, therefore, to urge upon you now is the urgent
necessity of your leaving Cornwall, and
coming up at once to town; for it is not
here, as I have hinted to you, but only in
London, that you can expect to meet with
a suitable *parti*.'

'Now I wonder what the wicked old
wretch can mean by *that?*' thought Susan
Ramsay.

' Of   course,'   returned   Gwendoline
coldly ; ' " that goes without saying." '

' Well, I want *you* to go without saying—that is, without saying anything to
the contrary,' said the baronet peevishly.
' I detest argument and bother, and I
know so very much better what is good for
you than you do yourself.   You will get
no good by being here any longer.   You

can't hide yourself away from the world of fashion for an indefinite time, and then come out again like a *débutante*, and carry all before you, as you did last year. If you do not hold the position that you have once secured for yourself, another, believe me, will step into your place, whom it may be difficult to oust.'

'You speak of the belle of the season as if she were a crossing-sweeper, papa,' said Gwendoline with a quiet smile.

'Never mind the homeliness of the metaphor, my dear; the fact is exactly as I have stated it. You must cease playing nursery-maid to that little brat yonder, and sick-nurse to Mrs Ferrier, and return with me to town next week.'

'I cannot leave Glen Druid so abruptly, papa,' answered Gwendoline gravely; 'but I promise you I shall remain with Mrs Ferrier not much longer, though I don't know exactly how long, or short, the time may be.'

'Why, I heard you, and I must say to my amazement, making plans with her only yesterday for accompanying her in the spring to Rome.'

Gwendoline looked cautiously about her, and once more sent her easily pleased little playmate for a long run after her sisyphean toy. Susan, keeping her body well concealed, craned forward eagerly, so as to lose no word of the coming communication, the importance of which showed itself even in Miss Treherne's calm and composed face.

'Mrs Ferrier will never see Rome,' said Gwendoline in low but distinct tones; 'she will never set foot again on her native soil.'

'Good heavens!' ejaculated Sir Guy with genuine horror; for the idea of death, even when it did not concern himself, was obnoxious to him as vulgarity itself. 'You don't mean to say she is going to die! Pooh! it don't kill every

woman to have a baby, although it killed
your poor dear mother: a beautiful delicate creature she was—quite unfit for that
sort of thing. Mrs Ferrier, to be sure,
does not seem very strong, but—'

'She is a doomed woman,' interrupted
Gwendoline solemnly. 'Nobody knows it
but Dr Gisborne and myself. But so it is:
when the baby is born, she will die—that
is quite certain.'

'Why, bless my soul, then it might
happen any day!' ejaculated Sir Guy,
reflecting instantly how very disagreeable
the occurrence of an incident of that kind
under the same roof with him would be,
and deciding in his own mind to receive a
letter the next morning which should require his presence in Pall Mall at once.

'Yes, it might happen any day; and
it *must* happen within a month or so,' said
Gwendoline coldly.

'It does not seem to disturb *you* much,'
observed Sir Guy involuntarily, for he was

really staggered at his daughter's *sang-
froid*.

'No, papa; I am not easily disturbed
by other people's misfortunes,' returned
she. 'I have my own affairs to look to;
and as you have so often told me, one's
own affairs, even when they are little ones,
are of more interest than the great ones
of other people. Besides, if I cannot credit
your excellent training with the whole of
my philosophy, I am accustomed to the
idea of what is about to happen: I have
known the truth for many weeks. When I
have taken my friend's feverish hand, and
kissed her hectic cheek at morn and eve,
I have often said to myself: Shall I ever
do this again? or when I next touch them,
will they be cold and dead?'

'What a dreadful notion!' exclaimed
the baronet, with a movement of disgust.
'I am sure I am sincerely sorry for the
poor woman, and grieved, for my friend
Ferrier's sake. I know what it is to lose

a wife myself. But, as I cannot possibly be of any use here, and, in fact, should be very much in the way— Should I not, Gwendoline, eh, now?'

'Certainly, papa, you would be of no use here in case anything happened to Giulia; and I think you would be quite right to leave Glen Druid.'

'You do, do you? Well, that is quite my view. If I could be of any possible service—but then I can't; now you— would *you* be prepared to go with me, Gwendoline, in case any important business should make it necessary for me to leave to-morrow—or how?'

'I shall stay here, papa,' said Gwendoline firmly, 'till all is over.'

'Now, there you are right again, my dear. I like to see women behave kindly and friendly towards one another—it's a thousand pities they don't always do it. Yes, yes; you'll stay; and there will be no necessity for my coming down again here to fetch you, will there? If the railway had got here, it would be different; but posting comes so devilish expensive, don't you see?'

'I understand the situation exactly, papa; and the other situation also about which we spoke at first. Believe me, I am quite prepared for the inconveniences to which I must necessarily be subjected by remaining here; and I do not wish you to share them. All I ask is, that you keep what I have told you a profound secret—that is absolutely necessary for more than one reason.'

'My dear Gwendoline, I will be silent as the gra— I mean, as the Warrior's Helm yonder; you may depend upon me for that, since I never speak upon such disagreeable matters at all. I am almost sorry that you mentioned the thing; and yet anything is better than to have had it happen while I was— Dear me, and Dr Gisborne came yesterday without my sleep-

ing-pills: I don't know what I shall do
to night without my pills.'

'Some one shall be sent at once to St
Medards for them,' said Gwendoline quietly.—'And now, Marion, my darling, I
think we must go in, for dear mamma will
be expecting us.'

And so the old man and the young
girl and the child, went up the steps together, and by the arbour—from which but
a few minutes before the hidden listener
had fled, with pallid cheeks and beating
heart—and found Mr Ferrier himself at
the front-door, who asked, in cheerful tones,
whether Miss Gwendoline did not think it
would 'do' for Giulia to take a drive that
morning, while the sunshine lasted, since,
in his opinion, there was 'nothing like
fresh air for setting a lady up when she
was a little ailing.'

CHAPTER X.

WE have said that Susan Ramsay was by nature reticent, except when she allowed herself the pleasure of conversing upon the topic of Mr Samuel Barland; but she had also the gift of preaching, or, at all events, of reproving evil-doers in ministerial language, in quite a remarkable degree, and enjoyed the exercise of it exceedingly. It was therefore with the utmost difficulty that she restrained herself for four-and-twenty hours from giving a piece of her mind to Miss Gwendoline Treherne respecting the wicked duplicity of her con-

duct with regard to her poor mistress. But
although she felt moved to this so strongly,
and her conscience even reproached her
with some cowardice as she thought of the
injunction 'to reprove, rebuke, in season
and out of season,' prudential reasons restrained a while her righteous indignation.
It was advisable, in the first place, to wait
until her two enemies were reduced to one,
which happened at noon on the next day,
through the departure of Sir Guy—a step
necessitated by a summons to town of the
last importance, which had arrived by that
morning's post. Her master, and even
her mistress, accompanied the baronet to
the hall steps; and she saw from an upper
window the hypocritical old wretch take
the latter's hand, and raising it to his lips,
express a hope that the next time he had
the pleasure of seeing her, she might be
quite well and strong; then he kissed his
daughter's cheek, and bade her take the
greatest care of their dear hostess, or he

should never forgive her; and then there
was a long warm leave-taking with shrewd,
but unsuspicious Mr Ferrier—the Mammon
of Unrighteousness, as he had called him—
which Susan, who 'could not abide such
falseness,' had not the patience to see
out, but drew her head in, and shook it
menacingly at wickedness in high places
generally, with a particular reference to
the Trehernes of Bedivere.

But even now that Sir Guy was gone, no
opportunity offered itself for some hours
for the deliverance of Susan's testimony
against his daughter, since her good sense
told her that that must be done without a
witness. Miss Treherne was far too self-
contained a foe to be attacked with mere
vehemence and indignation before a third
party, with whom one dexterous but quiet
parry might seem to put the assailant in
the wrong; so she waited, with quick beating heart and ire suppressed, throughout
that day, even until her mistress had re-

tired to her boudoir preparatory to going to bed. Thither, as often happened while Susan ministered unto her, came Gwendoline, also in her dressing-gown, to have a cosy chat with her dear Giulia; and this was, of all that had happened that day, the severest trial to the justly indignant waiting-maid; for the conversation of the pair, to which she had per force to listen, turned upon their plans and projects for that coming spring, which the one was so well aware that the other would never see. To hear her poor mistress talk with such gaiety and fervour of her native land, and of how she was certain she should be quite herself again if once she could breathe its warm blue air, was sad and pitiful enough; but when she came (as she did) to take such thought of that bright future as to picture the fair scenes they would visit in company, a grave slow voice interrupted her suddenly: 'Boast not thyself of to-morrow, dear mistress, for thou knowest not what a day may bring forth.'

'What does she mean—what *does* this woman mean?' asked Mrs Ferrier, looking with frightened face at Gwendoline.—'Why do you interrupt me, Susan, with such dreadful words?'

'It is only her Scotch way,' said Gwendoline in Italian. 'These puritans cannot resist the temptation to quote a text, and especially when it tends to turn one's happy thoughts into melancholy. It is nothing more, darling: do not mind her.'

Susan did not speak again; she did not, of course, know what Gwendoline had said to her mistress, but the use of the foreign tongue was a humiliation to her (as it always is to those who do not understand it when it is understood by others), and she felt that her imprudence had already put her at a disadvantage. She would be silent henceforth, if she had to hold her tongue with her teeth. But no further ordeal had to be undergone. Her late re-

mark, brief as it had been, had shaken the
nerves of her fragile mistress, and indis-
posed her for further talk.

'I am going to bed,' said she with
childish peevishness; 'and I have no further need of you, Susan, to-night. If you
have anything else to say that is unpleasant to listen to, keep it till I feel a little
stronger, please.—Good-night, Gwendoline, dear. How I love you, and wish
everybody else was like you in this cold,
harsh England; then, perhaps, I could
bear to live in it.' With a lingering, loving embrace she took leave of her friend,
and retired to her own room, which was at
the end of a little corridor, and not, as
usual, immediately next the boudoir.

Susan, though sincerely attached to her
mistress, was not one whose feelings were
easily 'hurt;' but the indignation within
her did not lessen to see herself in such
disfavour, and Gwendoline held in such
affection. It almost seemed to her, as she

now looked at her beautiful foe, that she
must be a witch such as the Scriptures
spoke of, who, by her magical charms,
could steal even human hearts, though it
was clear enough, by the expression of the
waiting-maid's face, that they had not
stolen *hers*.

'Your mistress has left these flowers
behind her,' observed Gwendoline; 'I
know she meant to take them with her.'
For such was Giulia's passionate love for
flowers that a bouquet of them always
stood opposite her dressing-table glass, so
that she could see them double—flower
and reflection, from her pillow. It was
not a healthy practice, for flowers absorb
the air, but 'What did it signify,' Dr
Gisborne said, 'since they pleased the poor
doomed lady.'

'Stop a moment, Miss Treherne,' said
the waiting-maid firmly, as Gwendoline
took up the vase and was about to follow

Mrs Ferrier; 'I have got a word or two to say to you.'

So far as Susan's news went—the information that she knew of her mistress's state of health, and also that Gwendoline was aware of it—her face had already betrayed it to her shrewd adversary.

'You are irritated, Susan,' said she smoothly, 'because Mrs Ferrier loves me, and chooses to show it; but it is foolish to be angry with me for what I cannot help. Nor must you be annoyed with your mistress for her sharp words, for, indeed, she is far from well, and when she speaks so, it is not from harshness, but from inward pain.'

This half avowal of the true state of the case was not only adapted to weaken the force of the accusation she foresaw was coming, but the long sentence also gave her time, while she was framing it, to consider how the charge could possibly have arisen. The idea, however, that her conversation with Sir Guy upon the terrace on the previous morning had been overheard, did not occur to her.

'Oh, I am not annoyed with my poor mistress, madam; and I know now, *as well as you have known all along*, how much she suffers, and what the end of it all needs must be.'

'Then you should be more careful, my good Susan, not to distress her with ill-timed remarks, such as the one to which you gave utterance just now. Rest and ease are all that are to be hoped for in her case, Dr Gisborne says, and we should do our best to give them to her.'

'That is a very wicked way of talking,' retorted Susan, though not without consciousness that the remark was by no means equal to the occasion. It was unintelligible, even to her, *how* the wind had been taken out of her sails; but here they were flapping idly against the mast, and the whole vessel of her wrath well-nigh becalmed. She had feared for the very force of the hurricane of indignation upon which she expected to be borne, and lo! it was now a matter of difficulty to her to be indignant enough. She seemed, indeed, to have been herself in fault, rather than the other, who thus talked of Mrs Ferrier's desperate condition as though it were a thing well known, and treated by all with delicate consideration. 'A very wicked way, I say,' reiterated Susan, ' of talking, and of acting too, Miss Treherne. It is all very well for Dr. Gisborne, who has only the body in view; but have we not all our responsibilities as regards one another's immortal souls? If the grave were the end of us, your conduct might perhaps be excusable. Is it the part of a Christian woman—for I suppose you do call yourself that—and one who pretends to be her friend too, to let a poor doomed creature sink and sink, without even so much as knowing of her danger, into what may (for all we know) be the bottomless pit? Think of the weeks she has spent in frivolous pleasures—how you, knowing what you did, could share in them, far less propose them, I can't think; but God is your judge, not me—when they might have been passed in preparing herself, as well as she could, poor ignorant soul, for *Death*. How could you do it, Miss Treherne?—how *dared* you do it? And to see you look so calm, and smile so sweet, when my dear mistress talks of getting well and strong.'

'No doctor is infallible; and who knows but that she will get well?' interrupted Gwendoline in firm unruffled tones.

'*You* know it!' exclaimed Susan, raising her voice and hand in passionate protest against such hypocrisy. 'You and your father know it, if no one else! To hear him wish her Good-bye this morning, and say, "We shall soon meet again, you know—" as I heard him say—sent quite a chill through me. Yet even he is not so false, and not so cruel, as were you just now. To lead her on, poor soul! to dream such dreams as never, never could be realized—to flatter her with prospects of blue skies, when long before the time comes that she pictures, she will be lying in the cold dark tomb, and as likely as not with her dead babe beside her—'

'Hush, fool!' cried Gwendoline imperiously; but the warning came too late. At the half-opened door stood the very subject of their talk, with her large eyes glaring out of their deep sockets, and her thin face damp with the dews of terror. She had come back almost at once for her vase of flowers, and overheard the whole of their discourse. Doomed woman as she was, she looked far worse than doomed —half-dead already—as, leaning against the door-way, she gazed from one to the other in an agony of speechless fear. The next moment she uttered a long wailing shriek (it seemed to Susan like the despairing cry of a lost soul), and before either Gwendoline or the waiting-maid could prevent her, fell heavily upon the floor.

That frightful cry aroused the house; Mr Ferrier himself rushed up-stairs, only to find his wife unconscious of his presence. They had placed her in her bed, where she lay in stupor, staring vacantly at the flowers which Gwendoline had not forgotten to put in their usual place. It flashed through the latter's mind that it might not be yet too late to conceal the peril of Mrs Ferrier's condition from her husband, and that even she herself might be persuaded, when she came to consciousness, to believe that all she had overheard was but the product of her own disordered fancy. Might not Susan, whose intemperate zeal had certainly caused the mischief, be disposed, from fear of the consequences to herself, to accede to this course of proceeding? But a look at the waiting-maid's set face convinced Gwendoline that she could not count upon her as an ally, and therefore she at once decided upon treating her as a foe.

When Mr Ferrier, with Giulia's cold unanswering fingers clasped in his, inquired hoarsely how all this had happened, Gwendoline pointed quietly to the waiting-maid, and said: 'That woman's folly has wrought it all. She meant no harm (I will say that for her even now); but she was so imprudent as to express her belief that Mrs Ferrier would not survive the birth of her babe, within her hearing; and Heaven grant that her prophecy may not have brought with it its own fulfilment!'

'Is this true, woman?' asked Mr Ferrier hoarsely—not that he had the least doubt of Gwendoline's word, but because the love of justice, which was very strong in him, mechanically suggested the inquiry.

'Yes, master, it is true, in a sense,' said poor Susan; 'but—'

'Leave this room, where you have done mischief enough, woman!' returned Mr Ferrier imperatively; 'and never set foot in it again.'

Loving fears for her mistress, and pity for her master, were filling Susan's honest heart: the sight of them before her faithful eyes—the one in a swoon, from which she might never awake; the other, haggard and sorrow-stricken, and looking already five years older since he had entered the room—overcame her utterly, and for the present swept from her mind all thought of combat with her foe, and even of self-justification. 'O sir,' said she with passionate earnestness, 'your dear wife is a dying woman; if I have unknowingly done her harm, forgive me, for it was for her poor soul's sake. For God's sake, speak to her of that, if in His mercy He again should give her ears to hear!'

' I *think* she had better leave the room, Mr Ferrier,' said Gwendoline, with a significant look towards his wife, into whose eyes consciousness was evidently slowly returning.

' If she does not, I will put her out by the shoulders,' exclaimed Mr Ferrier angrily.—' Go, mischievous tattler, and never again shall you see the mistress whom you have so injured ! '

' God forgive you, master, as I do ! ' said Susan meekly, ' and keep you,' added she, with a steady look at Gwendoline, ' from all designers and deceivers ! I have done my duty here in *His* sight, if not in yours.'

But Mr Ferrier heeded not her words; he only knew that she had obeyed his bidding and left the room. His thoughts were solely occupied with the fragile form that lay before him gasping painfully, but now returning the pressure of his fingers sensibly enough. Gwendoline guessed by her frightened eyes that she was holding fast to him for protection from that shadowy Pursuer, from whom there is no safety in the centre of an armed host; and even her husband was stricken with a vague dread that such was the case. 'Let Dr Gisborne be sent for instantly,' whispered he.

'That was done at once,' said Gwendoline quietly. 'I heard the messenger gallop off five minutes ago.'

'You think of everything,' said Mr Ferrier gratefully.

And indeed Gwendoline was thinking of a good many things just then: how she should excuse herself, when the time for explanation should come, for not having told him of his wife's condition—how she should excuse herself to Giulia. But mainly she was endeavouring to recall her yesterday's interview with her father, to which Susan's reference to Sir Guy had shown she had been a witness. What had she said about Piers? and how far, if at

all, had she compromised herself with respect to Mr Ferrier? Some expression
she surely must have used in connection
with him; or what did Susan mean by
'*designers* and deceivers?' But perhaps,
after all, that was only a random shaft of
the waiting-maid's, loosed from the string
of her tongue, in Parthian fashion, as she
fled the battle.

In the mean time, her friend and hostess was agitated by far other apprehensions.
Plots and plans, her simple, child-like mind
had never entertained; but now it had done
for ever even with its harmless schemes of
pleasure.

'Why do you look so frightened, dear
Giulia?' inquired her husband tenderly.
'There is no one here but me and your
friend Gwendoline. What ails you, darling?'

'Death! Death!' was the passionate
reply that burst from her fevered lips.
'It is Death I fear! It is Death I feel!

They have deceived me: I shall never see
Italy—never, never! I shall be lying, as
Susan said, "in the cold dark tomb" instead, with my dead babe lying beside
me!'

Gwendoline smiled compassionately:
unutterable pity and sorrow seemed to overcome her endeavours to look cheerful.
'Susan was very wrong and very foolish,
dear Giulia,' said she: 'we must not take
everything an ignorant woman says for
gospel.'

'Gospel, gospel!' murmured the sick
woman; 'that is what she is always talking about. O dear, O dear! Let a priest
be sent for at once, Bruce—a priest of my
own faith.'

It would have been difficult in every
sense to gratify the unhappy Giulia's desire, for in the first place there was no
Catholic priest within a score of miles;
and in the second, she had no faith of her
own, to call such, of any kind. Her

father's religion, composed at best half of
Superstition, half of Art, the poor girl had
imbibed from him at second-hand; but her
early marriage and removal to England
had erased its impressions from her mind,
on which, as on a palimpsest, the creed of
her husband, or rather of Susan, had been
since as vaguely inscribed. Her soul was
shaken by Calvinistic terrors, while her
thin hand was mechanically making the
sign of the cross upon her bosom, and her
tongue reiterating, 'Send for a priest,
Bruce—send for a priest.'

'Dr Gisborne has been sent for, darling,' said Gwendoline softly; and instantly a ray of comfort shone upon that
troubled face.

'Thanks, thanks!' she murmured.
'He is good as well as wise; he is a priest
and a physician in one; and perhaps, since
he is so clever, perhaps he may save me
even still.'

CHAPTER XI.

'I NEVER EVEN HEARD OF THE PEOPLE.'

IT would be painful as well as unnecessary to dwell further upon poor Giulia's illness and distress of mind. Dr Gisborne came as soon as the message from Glen Druid reached him, which was as quickly as the man could get to St Medards; for that physician was not an ordinary country doctor, liable to be called hither and thither, and always away when wanted on an emergency, but only attended a few families, and that quite as much for his pleasure as his profit, notwithstanding that his gratuitous services were ever at the

service of the poor. He had guessed from
what he had gathered from the groom,
that the crisis of Mrs Ferrier's fate must
be at hand, and he made up his mind to
face her husband's possible displeasure
—for the doctor had had his doubts of the
rectitude of his own silence—for having
concealed from him his wife's state of
health. His satisfaction was therefore
considerable at finding, on his arrival, that
his favourite Gwendoline had already
smoothed that matter over for him, and
taken the blame upon her own shoulders.
She had made the confession with quiet
frankness to Mr Ferrier himself, as they
sat together watching Giulia, who, worn
out with feverish excitement, had fallen
into a short sleep, from which her husband
was already drawing a favourable augury.

' How came that stupid woman to take
it into her head that Giulia was so ill, I
wonder?' said he, as much in soliloquy as
in interrogation.

'I am afraid that was my fault, Mr Ferrier,' said Gwendoline softly. 'I was indiscreet enough to let her know that your sweet wife was in a very perilous state.'

'Perilous you mean, of course, as respects her condition?'

'Hush! no; I wish I did. Dr Gisborne informed me some time since that we could not hope to have her with us for many months.'

'Good God! Miss Treherne, what are you saying?'

'Alas, only the truth, Mr Ferrier.'

'And why, in Heaven's name, has this been kept a secret from me, whom it concerned the most?'

'For that very reason, dear Mr Ferrier. If anybody is to blame, blame me. Dr Gisborne was in doubt as to whether he should tell you all or not, and I persuaded him to be silent. It is not as if you could possibly have anything to reproach yourself

with. Another husband might have had moments of irritation or displeasure with his
wife, for which, now that he saw her thus,
his conscience would reproach him; but with
you, who are all patience and indulgence,
this, I knew, could never be the case.
Moreover, your very love for her was such,
I argued, that you could not have concealed from your darling the knowledge of
the calamity that was overhanging her;
and the disclosure would at once have produced the catastrophe which we see here,
and which has, in fact, been brought about
in the way I feared.'

The rare tears stood in Mr Ferrier's
eyes as he gazed upon his fair young wife
with that yearning love which we only
feel when we perceive the certainty of its
object being taken away from us; and
the sigh he uttered seemed a farewell to all
hope.

Gwendoline did not venture to breathe
a word of pity; she did not even touch

his arm with that slight pressure of the
fingers which, in moments of sorest sorrow,
may bring, if not the balm of sympathy,
at least a 'moment's distraction of our
thoughts, in the remembrance that a friend
and well-wisher is by. She for once dis-
carded the weapons of her charms, feeling
that at such a time they would win her
nothing, and finished what she had to say
in calm collected tones, in which lay
neither apology nor tenderness.

'I am sorry the course I thought it
best to take has displeased you, dear Mr
Ferrier, but I am not surprised. When
misfortune comes, it always seems that we
might have been better prepared to meet
it. It only remains for me now to make
amends, as far as in me lies, for my tres-
pass against you, by devotion to our dear
one.'

'Yes, yes; you will stay with us,
Gwendoline, I know,' sighed the old man;
'you will not desert us in our hour of trial.'

She knew that he was unaware he had
called her by her Christian name, but his
having done so gratified her, nevertheless,
as did his other words, although they
also were spoken half mechanically. The
one convinced her how familiar to the
mind of her host her presence had become; the other how necessary she had
made herself to him and his. She had
not mentioned to him the second argument
for silence which she had used with Dr
Gisborne, because she foresaw that he—if
only in gratitude for her having taken the
blame upon herself—would certainly reveal
it to Mr Ferrier; and so it presently happened.

In the long private talk that ensued,
after the physician had seen his patient,
between the husband and himself, the
latter told the former that Gwendoline had
begged him to keep Giulia's disease a
secret, to save Mr Ferrier pain. ' Besides
the risk of hastening the calamity—such

were her very words—why make her good husband wretched before his time?'

'That was at least kind and thoughtful of her,' said Mr Ferrier; 'and I am sure I forgive her from my heart. She has been a sunbeam in this house for weeks, doctor; and now that all is gloom, she seems to shine the brighter.'

'And yet there are folks who say that she is cold-hearted,' said the physician indignantly, 'and only cares for fashion and frivolity. I happen to know that she might have been all this time in town (and indeed Sir Guy pressed her to go thither), the idol of that world to which she is said to be devoted; but she told me that she felt her place to be here with her sick friend—as it will be, Mr Ferrier, I am certain, until the end.'

And the end was not destined to be very far off. After giving premature birth to a little daughter, poor Giulia

passed out of the world, for which she
was so little suited, with a gentle smile.
Her terrors had all departed, and with her
last breath she whispered to her husband
that she saw her dear Italy before her, and
that she was going there after all. Her
affection for Gwendoline seemed to have
met with some sudden check, for she neither caressed nor addressed her. She gave
no explanation of this change in her feelings, nor did Mr Ferrier, rapt in his great
grief, observe it; and it was Gwendoline
who ministered to her to the last, and
whose arms raised little wondering Marion
to the bedside to take her mother's farewell.
In one particular only did Mr Ferrier
show himself not utterly overwhelmed
with the fact of his bereavement—he was
resolute in his determination to dismiss
Susan Ramsay, at whose door he persisted
in laying the catastrophe, or, at all events,
the hastening of it; and with characteris-

tic firmness, he paid her what was due to her with his own hands, and, as it happened, in Gwendoline's presence.

Susan, dissolved in genuine tears, had not a word to say in mitigation of her master's wrath; she was not thinking of herself at all, for indeed further service was no object to her, but only of her dead mistress and of her darling Marion, from whom it deeply grieved her to part.

'Is that your just due, woman?' inquired Mr Ferrier sternly, putting her money with the extra month's wage, in default of warning, into her hand.

'Yes, sir; and I thank you for all your kindness,' sobbed Susan. 'I have only one favour to ask you more—that I may see my dear dead mistress once before I go.'

'Never!' said Mr Ferrier vehemently. 'That shall be your punishment. She forgave you; and I, for—yes, I forgive you, and that is enough.'

'O sir,' cried Susan, 'anger should not

last beyond the grave; and I did love her so; pray, let me.'

Mr Ferrier's iron face relaxed; her unexpected tears and tone were softening him.

'If my intervention may have any weight at all, dear Mr Ferrier,' said Gwendoline appealingly, 'I pray you put it in the scale of mercy. I entreat you to let this faithful, if mistaken woman have her wish.'

Susan drew herself up quickly, and her black eyes flashed through her tears. 'I am speaking to my master, miss, and want no grace from you, nor never shall.'

'Excuse me, Miss Treherne,' said Mr Ferrier angrily, 'but I cannot suffer your unfailing kindness to be thus abused. Not another word I beg.—And you, Susan, you insolent coarse woman—whom I shall not stoop to tell how this honoured young lady has spoken on your behalf before—leave my house at once; and never darken its doors again.'

So Susan Ramsay, in disgrace, betook herself to St Medards, to dwell for the present with Mr Sam Barland's mother, not only until such time as the banns could be put up, and their little arrangements made for marriage, but for a considerable interval in addition, which Susan insisted upon, as a mark of respect to the memory of that dear mistress of whom she had been so harshly forbidden to take farewell. And to this arrangement Mr Samuel Barland, who was a philosopher, as well as a man of science, unresistingly assented.

The news of the catastrophe at Glen Druid was carried, in black-bordered missives, to no numerous yet to widely different circles. To Miss Judith Ferrier, the widower's only sister, for instance, who had her habitation in her native Glasgow; and to Sir Guy Treherne, who had his lodgings over his club, on the shady side of Pall Mall. Also to the Honourable Piers Mostyn at Stonegate Hall, Yorkshire, whom it reached in rather a strange fashion.

The rest of the men who were staying in the house had gone hunting that morning, but he himself being more a squire of dames than a fox-hunter, was starting for a ride with two of the ladies, when the post arrived, and brought him a letter addressed in Gwendoline's hand. He had had no word from her—although she had promised to keep him acquainted with her movements—since that night of his dismissal from Bedivere Court; and he opened the envelope with enough of agitation to make the keen eyes that were slily watching him twinkle with merriment. Could Sir Guy be dead, and had she written, in her loneliness and poverty, to say that she would wed him, as he had pressed her to do? There was not a line of her handwriting within, but only two slips, cut out of a Cornish newspaper. ' *On the 24th inst., at Glen Druid, the wife of Bruce Fer-*

rier, Esq., of a daughter.' And culled from the death-column of the same paper, the following : *' On the 25th inst., Giulia, the beloved wife of Bruce Ferrier, Esq., of Glen Druid.'*

Piers Mostyn muttered an oath beneath his breath. Confound the girl ! What did she mean by sending him that sentimental rubbish, as though this dead woman had been her dearest friend ? Of course she only did so as an excuse for her long silence ; but she was foolish indeed if she supposed that such a subterfuge would impose upon *him.* 'The Ferriers of Glen Druid ? Why, I never even heard of the people.'

THE RIPENING.

CHAPTER XII.

GWENDOLINE TELLS PAPA.

THERE is no occupation in which (to honest eyes) a young girl looks so attractive as when she is ministering to the happiness of children; and this is more especially the case when those children have no protectress of their own. Gwendoline, although retiring nightly to Bedivere Court, passed her days, as before, at Glen Druid, devoting herself to little Marion and the baby, with the former of whom, at least, she filled, and more than filled, the place of her dead mother; for

the late Mrs Ferrier had not really pos-
sessed the stamina requisite for the per-
formance of the duties of head of a family,
far less of a great household ; and the wi-
dowed husband, despite his grief, could not
help observing how much more smoothly
matters were ruled under the new dynasty,
than when the ' exotic,' as poor Giulia had
nicknamed herself, was mistress of his
house.   If it had not been for the children,
Gwendoline would not, of course, have
had the shadow of an excuse for revisiting
the place after her friend's death ; but
their motherless condition was for the present her warrant, while they themselves
afforded always a subject of conversation
with her host, and the means of escape
from all embarrassment, if, indeed, she
ever felt any.

A tranquil sigh or two over the fate of
the bright flower which death had snatched
from them ; and a few words of eulogy, or
modestly tendered counsel, regarding the

small tenants of the nursery, were all that
Gwendoline herself ventured to utter at
their solitary meals; she initiated no other
topic whatever; but after a time, Mr Ferrier began, as usual, to converse with her
upon business matters, and with greater
frankness than ever. In particular, he
talked to her with perfect unreserve concerning his property, which she learned,
without surprise, produced an income of
nearly thirty thousand pounds a year. He
was not by nature addicted to horse or
carriage exercise; and since the neighbours had not been very congenial with
his late wife, he had kept much at home,
so that he had already been thrown into
Gwendoline's society far more than is
generally the case with host and guest of
their respective ages; and now, when he
was restricted by his recent calamity more
than ever to his own roof and grounds,
there was scarce an hour in the day that
he passed out of the comforting sunshine

of her presence. Nevertheless, Mr Ferrier could not rid himself of scruple with respect to Gwendoline's tarry at Glen Druid, so easily as she did. Respectability was an important part of his religion, and to outrage it, was in itself a species of blasphemy, in which, however pleasant, he could not permit himself to indulge. Moreover, there was Gwendoline's own reputation to be considered. Of course, the idea of anything unpleasant or malicious being said of her, had never entered into her innocent head: wrapped up in the memory of her dear friend, and in her devotion to those left, but for her own tender solicitude, to a hireling's care, she had never given a thought to what the world might say; it was therefore all the more incumbent upon him to lay before her, as delicately as he could, the true state of the case; a difficult duty enough, since, in the first place, it required rather tender handling; and in the second (although he did not know it), Gwendoline had fully made up her mind to misunderstand him. The arrival, however, of a letter from his sister at Glasgow, gave Mr Ferrier the long-looked-for, though scarcely desired, opportunity of unburdening his conscience upon this matter.

'My dear Miss Treherne,' said he, 'I have been thinking as to whether it would not be advisable to ask Judith to come and stay at Glen Druid.'

Gwendoline opened her large eyes, and with a smile, almost the first which she had yet ventured to wear, replied: 'I am most pleased to hear it, Mr Ferrier. It seems a pity you should be so long estranged from your only living relative; and, to say truth, I had always entertained an idea that there was not the cordial feeling between you—though I am sure the fault does not lie with one so kindly as yourself—which should always exist between brother and sister.'

'Nay; Judith is an excellent woman in her way, though she is somewhat narrow and prejudiced in her views. We always got on together very well—until of late years.'

'Is it possible, then, that she could find anything amiss with your poor lost darling?' said Gwendoline with innocent indignation.

'Not "amiss" exactly, for that, as you hint, would be impossible. But Judith has always lived in the north, and among her own people; she had a sort of horror, I fancy, of all foreigners, and disapproved altogether of my marriage.'

'You did not ask her leave, however, I suppose?' said Gwendoline, again smiling.

'No, indeed,' returned Mr Ferrier, with a flush upon his grave shrewd face. 'I have, throughout my life, been my own master in all respects. But my union with Giulia produced a coolness between myself and Judith. You, however, who have such tact, and—and—who make yourself so pleasant to everybody, would find no difficulty, I am sure, in getting on with my sister: she is a little stiff and formal, but she has really a good heart, and—and—'

'My dear Mr Ferrier,' interrupted Gwendoline quietly, 'you may be quite certain that I should do my best to be courteous and respectful to any one so nearly related to yourself as the lady in question. I could easily forgive her any such defects as you mention; and would very gladly submit, for your sake, to any wholesome reproof with which she might please to visit my unregenerate self. But what I can *not* forgive—and if I could, what I could not be able to forget, so that it must needs (I feel) influence my behaviour towards Miss Ferrier, in spite of myself—is her dislike of my sweet friend, your late beloved wife. I quite understand the course of training, and the social associations which may have caused your sister to regard Giulia as she did; it may not have been her fault at all, but only her misfortune, yet I cannot—indeed, I cannot —in justice to that dear memory, consent to treat as my friend the woman who so misjudged her.'

'I really don't know what is to be done, then,' said Mr Ferrier doubtfully. 'I was in hopes you might have contrived to get on with Judith; and I scarcely see, unless she comes here, how—I really think it would be advisable—' He stammered and hesitated, and for the first time, to Gwendoline's eyes, his rugged features wore an appealing and almost tender look. She instantly perceived that his proposal to invite his sister was mainly suggested by the idea that she herself might not only retain her present position at Glen Druid without impropriety, but be more constantly there even than before; and her heart beat with triumph to learn it.   Her tone, however, was quiet and cold enough, as she replied : ' I cannot understand your difficulty, my dear Mr Ferrier. There is surely no sort of reason why you should not invite your own sister to Glen Druid, especially now the innocent cause of her displeasure is no longer here.'

Mr Ferrier paused, and bit his lip. Gwendoline was purposely taking the course most calculated to make Judith intolerable to him : she had another shaft too in her quiver yet, and the time had come for her to let it fly. ' There is certainly one objection to Miss Ferrier's coming,' said she musingly, ' though it hardly becomes me to mention it, and I must ask you to forgive me the liberty, for the sake of the motive that prompts me to take it. Your darling Marion is growing of an age to understand the feelings as well as the mere spoken words of those about her ; and it would cut your loving heart to the core, sir—for I leave my own purposely

out of the question—if you should have
cause to think that your daughter should
be learning to despise her mother. I know
from Giulia's own lips that Miss Ferrier
was wont to regard her at the best—as a
papist and a foreigner—with pious horror.
Do you think it certain she may not in-
spire the child with similar feelings?
Marion has a most loving, but also a most
impressionable nature; and, for my own
part, I have done my best to guard it from
receiving the thought of harm—the idea
of contempt for anybody; but another and
more strong-minded teacher might soon
undo my poor lessons.'

'My dear Miss Treherne,' exclaimed
Mr Ferrier, earnestly, and as he spoke he
rose and took her hand in his, ' I can never
forget your kindness to me and mine. It
would indeed be a sad loss to all of us—all
that are left, that is—and to my little ones
in particular, should your kind face cease
to shine upon us at Glen Druid. But,

perhaps, if you were to consult Sir Guy
upon the matter, he is so perfectly con-
versant with all that the best society exacts
or expects—'

'Oh, I *see !*' ejaculated Gwendoline,
with a low musical laugh. 'How very,
very stupid you must have thought me,
Mr Ferrier ! I have, I now understand,
been setting at defiance the opinion of the
world, in being so much at Glen Druid.
The fact is,' added she with a sadder air,
' *my* world has been limited of late to those
two little ones above-stairs, and—and—to
yourself, Mr Ferrier.'

'I know that well, my dear Miss Treherne,' said the old man with emotion ;
'and Heaven knows how unwillingly I
have performed my duty in thus drawing
your attention to what, in itself most innocent and laudable, may yet possibly set in
motion the tongue of vulgar scandal.'

'Vulgar scandal, my dear Mr Ferrier,'
said Gwendoline haughtily, 'does not af-

fect me very seriously, though I thank you
for your warning, and appreciate it. I
would bear far more, for the sake of you
and yours, than the knowledge that the
good people at St Medards have expressed
an opinion adverse to my discretion. I
could undergo the reserve of its banker's
wife, and the cold-shoulder of its attorney's
daughter, and yet survive.' It was impossible to conceive a more graceful shape
of scorn than Gwendoline exhibited as she
pronounced those words with a sweep of
her stately arm, in the calm contempt of
which it almost seemed that Mr Ferrier
himself was included.

'It is very natural, my dear Miss Treherne,' said he hastily, 'that you, being
what you are, should despise such people
and their possible talk. I only hinted at
the matter because I saw that it had never
entered into your mind—as, indeed, why
should it do so? But it really would be a
relief to me—since I could never forgive

myself if your devotion to my little ones should expose you to the shadow of an imputation—if you would lay the matter before Sir Guy as I have ventured to put it before yourself.'

'I will do that, my dear Mr Ferrier, and in person; for papa, whether influenced by the same motive as yourself I know not, has, in this very note, written me to say that he is shortly about to return home.'

'But why should he not come *here*, instead of to Bedivere Court?' pleaded Mr Ferrier. 'Why should you not both come here, and stay as before? It would be so kind of you to take pity on my loneliness; and—little Marion would be *so* pleased.'

And thus it happened that Sir Guy and his daughter became once more located at Glen Druid, nominally as guests, but without any definite limit to the duration of their visit. Everything was made as pleasant for the old baronet as could be contrived. He had had his doubts about coming to stay at a place where anything so unpleasant· as death had recently occurred; and was pleased to express his approbation at the 'good sense' which characterized the chief mourner in abstaining from all allusion to the topic. Sir Guy looked upon the Great Calamity as a careful housewife regards a spot upon her carpet or her curtains—something to be erased, if possible, at once and altogether; but, if kept in memory, to be carefully put out of sight, and never hinted at. And these precautions were taken at Glen Druid with respect to its deceased mistress. No allusion to the melancholy topic was ever made in his presence; he ate and drank of the best; he rose and retired when it suited him; the resources of the establishment were placed as much at his own disposal as though it had been his own. But after a time he began to get tired, as usual, with even so favourable a specimen of country

life, and to pine for the pleasures of Picca-
dilly. This was excusable, or, at all events,
natural in Sir Guy's case; they were the
only pleasures, and, indeed, the only pursuits, that he had ever known; and though
they were less vivid than they had used to
be, in the absence of any other magnet
they were still attractive. The course of
a selfish voluptuary towards its close is—
with the substitution of one sort of work
for another—in many respects similar to
that of an agricultural labourer. The latter, with feebler powers, has to toil on at
precisely the same work to which he so
vigorously applied himself in his youth;
his trembling hands still wield the spade
or the hoe, although the return for his
labour has become so lamentably small : he
knows no other thing to do. And so the
ancient man of pleasure continues in his
scarcely less narrow groove, enjoying less
and less, but still doing his best to enjoy.
Now, Sir Guy, although he disliked all

mention of the fact, was secretly aware
that old age was creeping upon him, and
that he had not much time to waste in admiring, or pretending to admire, the picturesque in Cornwall. He had arrived at
the epoch when every year brings with it
a change that is felt in *loss*, and it was
most important to utilize what faculties yet
remained to him. It would be time enough,
when every capacity for pleasure was exhausted, to lie and stare at the sky and the
sea. But it was difficult to express these
sentiments to another with the perspicuity
with which they presented themselves to
his own mind, or, indeed, to express them
at all without incurring an imputation of
egotism beyond what even he was prepared
to bear. He proceeded, therefore, to at-
tribute his resolution to depart to the importance of time to his daughter, and the
necessity of her repairing with him to
London for her own sake. Moreover, he
was not without his suspicions of the part

which she was playing in respect to their host, the widower, and he willingly seized the opportunity of discovering how far they were correct. Thereupon, one bright warm day in early spring, upon that terraced walk on which Gwendoline had informed him of the approaching death of their late hostess, Sir Guy and his daughter had a second conversation together, only the latter took care that it should be on this occasion without an eavesdropper.

'I have been thinking a good deal lately of our stay here, Gwendoline,' said Sir Guy a little clumsily—for she purposely offered him no chance of gliding imperceptibly on to this topic—'and, upon my life, I think it ought to come to an end.'

'Do you think we are outstaying our welcome, papa?' inquired she coldly. 'Don't you get the same wine that you liked so much at first?'

'My dear Gwendoline, what a vulgar

notion! Of course everything is as it should be in that respect. To do Mr Ferrier justice, whatever money can buy—down here—he places at my disposal: his domestic expenditure, in fact, is princely; but I suppose his income fully justifies *that;*' and Sir Guy gave a sharp glance at his daughter.

'He has nearly thirty thousand pounds a year, papa; he told me so with his own lips.'

'Indeed! That is a large rent-roll, or rather, it is something better, for I fancy his fortune is invested in more valuable securities than fields and farms.'

'Yes; it is mostly in government stocks, and could be realized (if he wished to do so) to-morrow. Mr Ferrier has told me all about it.'

'So it seems, my dear,' said Sir Guy significantly. 'But, however rich our host may be, he is not a man to neglect his children. The channels which his wealth will flow in hereafter, are already marked out; so that, in my opinion, Gwendoline, you are wasting valuable time by staying down here.'

'I think not, papa.' Her tone was quiet and distinct, and the gaze with which she met Sir Guy's impatient glance was as steady as her tone.

'But I tell you, you *are*,' urged he. 'It is not only that you are losing here all opportunity of securing a suitable position in life, but you are also in some sort compromising yourself. I hinted, you know, by letter, at the inadvisability of your being here so much after Mrs Ferrier's death; and even now, though I am with you, our making so long a stay at Glen Druid must needs certainly provoke remark.'

'I will take the risk of that, papa. Thanks to your frankness months ago, I thoroughly understand my own affairs; I have looked at the situation from all points, I assure you.'

'Do you mean me to infer, Gwendoline, that the opportunities which a London season might afford are no longer of any consequence in your eyes—that you have made your plan in life altogether independent of them?'

'Just so, papa.'

He understood her at once; and upon the whole he was not displeased. Out of so large a fortune as Mr Ferrier's, there would doubtless be pickings for himself, as well as ample provision for his daughter: but yet so high was the opinion that he entertained—and justly—of the effect of Gwendoline's charms, that he could not help feeling that they might have been disposed of elsewhere to even still greater advantage.

'It is, as you say, your own affair, my dear Gwendoline,' mused Sir Guy—'quite your own affair. But, of course, I, as your father, cannot but feel a very deep interest in this matter; and it does strike me that your ambition is somewhat easily gratified; that you might have looked a little higher.'

She smiled and raised her eyebrows a hair-breadth.

'There is nothing objectionable in Mr Ferrier, it is true,' he continued; 'he is a gentleman, and knows how to behave him-self. But are you sure, my dear Gwendo-line, you are quite suited for the sort of humdrum life, which, as his wife, you must needs lead? Without the least offence to his excellent abilities—and they tell me he is a first-rate man of business—does it not occur to you that our admirable host is just a trifle dull? He will not get brighter, Gwendoline, as time goes on, remember that; and he is already, for a husband, an old man.'

'Yes, he is an old man,' said Gwendo-line.

The phrase was a mere reiteration of her father's words, but it was uttered in a tone of great significance. No other word was added; and Sir Guy, on his part, did but nod his head, to let her know that he quite comprehended her meaning.

CHAPTER XIII.

PIERS MOSTYN BECOMES RESTIVE.

IN accordance with the perfect mutual understanding which existed between Sir Guy and his daughter, and which is said to be so great a desideratum in those relations, not another word was hinted of the former's return to town. For the sake of his child, almost as much as for any profit that might accrue to himself out of her contemplated plan, the good baronet determined to make a sacrifice of the pleasures of the London Season. He may have been, and probably was, impatient in secret, but externally he was imperturbable.

He listened to Mr Ferrier's anecdotes of his early struggles after fortune with a calm despair, that the narrator took for admiring wonder, and heard with genuine interest the twice-told story of his success, for in the fruits of the latter he felt that he might have some share. He even, on one occasion, honoured with his presence the institution of family prayer; this condescension, however, was a failure, nature and art (in Sir Guy's legs and trousers) having equally incapacitated him from kneeling, while devotional monotone at once superinduced repose. The domestics trooped out of the room in suppressed hysterics, while Sir Guy with his face buried in his chair was in the land of dreams.

Whenever his daughter had had a few minutes' talk alone with their host, poor Sir Guy would cast a covert glance of inquiry towards her, to know whether all these sacrifices had met with their reward, or if he was still doomed to suffer on. But

although Mr Ferrier had as fully made up
his mind to propose to Gwendoline as
Gwendoline had to accept him, those ideas
of respectability, with which no amount of
fortune will permit men to dispense unless
they have also been brought up in good
society, delayed the declaration month
after month. It was almost time enough
—taking the conventional ' year and a day'
as the correct limit—for the widower to
marry again before he ventured to offer
himself in marriage.

The proposal was made in characteristic terms. He did not allude to his advanced time of life, to the disparity between their respective ages, at all; but he
told Gwendoline—and quite truly—that
however strange it might seem, she was
the only person who had ever inspired him
with what he imagined to be Love. He
had loved his late wife, he said, in the
sense that most persons could be content
to accept the word; but he had never ex-

perienced in her case those feelings of
respect, admiration, and worship which
were actuating him now. And yet he
confessed, that, even thus, he would have
forborne to declare himself, did he not feel
that in doing so he was endeavouring to
secure for his two children the kindest and
wisest guardian they could ever hope to
know.

And Gwendoline's reply, though she
was very careful not to wound the old
man's *amour propre*, dwelt upon the children also, to whom she modestly hoped she
might prove herself a nearer and dearer
relative than what is commonly suggested by the term of step-mother. There was
as little of protestation or appeal on the
one side, as there was of coyness or hesita-
tion on the other. The upshot of it all
took none in the household by surprise, and
scarcely any one in the neighbourhood.

When Sir Guy and his daughter departed for their own house, it was taken as a

sign by all the county that Glen Druid
would presently become more their home
than ever.

There was a certain letter despatched
from St Medards to Glasgow the next
morning describing the matter as fully
settled, and not at all as mere common
report.

' My DEAR MADAM,' it ran, ' the engagement of which I have always written to
you as certain to happen between your
brother and Miss Treherne has at last
taken place. I am myself surprised that
she did not cause him sooner to forget my
poor dear mistress; though it is early days
enough for him to think of wedding again,
goodness knows. It seems but the other
day that he sent for me, on your kind re-
commendation, to be her waiting-maid at
Glen Druid. Well, well, it is not my
good master's fault; she would hoodwink
the sharpest eyes that ever *man* wore—
though she never hoodwinked mine.

Heaven grant it may not turn out to be his misfortune! The wicked Sir Guy took his daughter back with him yesterday— until I suppose the marriage takes place— to Bedivere Court; else they have not been there, except for a day or two at a time, for months. For my part, I call such goings-on scarcely decent, but then I am only a poor person, who, it seems, is not fit to be a judge of what is right among people of quality. That is what my husband says, and one is bound to believe one's husband.

'In communicating this sad news, according to your request, directly I hear it, it is only right to add that all the folks at Glen Druid are agreed that Miss Treherne behaves well enough to the dear children —that is, *at present*. My sweet Marion was certainly very fond of her; but the fact is she comes over everybody, man, woman, and child, and, if folks were served as they deserve, would be burned as a

witch. There's Mr Alexander Blackett of
the Glen, for one, is said to be ready to
shoot himself because of this news; his
sister, who is a very proper-minded lady,
actually called at our shop for medicines
for him to-day; and yet Miss Treherne
can certainly never have given *him* much
encouragement. But then a smile from
her goes further with the men than' (here
some words had been carefully erased in
the manuscript, and the following written
over them)—' than the most excellent gifts
and pleasant discourse in another. Ah,
madam, and that reminds me how I envy
you in Glasgow, with such great opportunities of hearing the Truth from persuasive
preachers; we have none such in this
graceless place; and I doubt whether Mr
Ferrier has done much good in paying
for the ministry. The last tracts came safe
enough to hand, but I could not do much
with them. The door here is not yet open
wide enough. I blush to say that with the

Smoker's Fate my husband lit his pipe.
What good, however, might *you* not effect
by coming down hither in person! I suppose Mr Ferrier will bid you to the wedding. I can think of nothing else than
that; all my thoughts come round to it
again, whithersoever they wander. When
time and place are arranged, you shall
hear without fail, dear madam.—Yours
respectfully, SUSAN BARLAND.'

This was not the first letter, by many,
that Susan had written to her old patron-
ess and fellow-country-woman since her
summary dismissal from Glen Druid.
With all her faults and prejudices, Susan
had an honest heart, which nourished no
bitterness against her late master, and a
most passionate affection for little Marion.
Her mind was thoroughly made up as to
the character of Miss Treherne; and not
the most eloquent preacher in North
Britain could have persuaded her to take
a different view of it.

Miss Ferrier was not, upon the whole, displeased to learn that her brother had fallen the second time a victim to woman's wiles; it served him right for not having had his sister to live with him, who understood scheming hussies of all kinds so thoroughly, and would have protected him from their arts. The fact was, however, that Mr Ferrier and Judith had dwelt under the same roof together (though not at Glen Druid) for some years, until the latter, with her strait-laced ways and acid religion, had fairly driven him from it to Italy, and (as it happened) to Giulia. Perhaps the foreign painter's daughter had even proved more attractive to him from the complete contrast which she afforded to the honest and kind-hearted, but severe and oppressive, Scotchwoman. Judith was one of those uncompromising social despots who are always causing, or, at all events, precipitating, domestic revolutions, and yet remain totally unconscious of their

own folly: they lay all the fault at the
door of the rebels, whom they accuse, as
Charles I. did, ' of impatience of taxation ; '
and protest that, ' for their part, they have
nothing to reproach themselves with ; and
if the time came round again, they should
behave precisely the same—' which indeed
they would probably do.   It is these well-
meaning but impracticable folks — with
their opposites—who make one sometimes
think that the devil has stolen not only
' all the best tunes,' but all the best manners, tastes, and tempers also.   It was
curious, but also very characteristic, in
Judith Ferrier, that notwithstanding she
had received from Susan such an unflatter-
ing portrait of Gwendoline, she spent
several afternoons in driving about her
native town in triumph to inform her kins-
folk and acquaintance that Bruce was engaged to be married to an English baronet's daughter, who had been the belle of
a London Season.   Perhaps, however, it

was to recompense herself for the silence
she had been compelled to keep with respect to his first wife, concerning whom
and her antecedents she could only close
her eyes and hold up her hands.

All unconscious of the interest which
she was thus exciting in the great northern
city, Gwendoline was sitting at home
calmly receiving the congratulations of
her friends. The first step of her proposed
life-journey—or rather of the introduction
to it—had been safely accomplished, and
her future was secured. Under such circumstances, one might have supposed she
would have rested carelessly on her oars a
little, and drifted easily down the stream
that was bearing her to fortune. But she
was not at all at ease, and very far from
being without care. While her friends
were felicitating her upon the coming
event, and even her father was compli-
menting her on the success her prudence
had achieved, she felt by no means sure of

victory. At this supreme moment, when she had written him word that her proposed plan—or, as she wrote it, 'our plan'—was already bearing fruit, the patient Piers had turned restive and dangerous.

The Honourable Piers Mostyn was neither better nor worse than many men of his class, while in appearance he offered a favourable type of it. He took the same pains in his personal adornment and effect as any of them, and he had excellent native material to work upon. He was really a very handsome, if somewhat effeminate-looking, young gentleman, to begin with, and he was always faultlessly attired. What he would have looked like in corduroys and a bad hat—what would have become of all that *distingué* and aristocratic appearance *then*—can never be known. He never wore corduroys nor a bad hat. He had a very engaging smile, though it was only fascinating, and not genial; an insinuating address, and a musical voice devoid of drawl. But, except in attire and manners, he owed nothing to 'the long result of time;' the centuries behind him 'like a fruitful land reposed,' but they had borne no fruit, save in the above particulars, for *him*. He had no knowledge, no tastes (to be called such), no acquirement whatever, beyond the French language, which he spoke easily, and with a good accent. What his feelings might have been under more favourable circumstances, can never be known; all his moral machinery had been 'brutalized' very early, and was now hopelessly out of gear. Although but the younger son of a poor peer, he had breathed the incense of flattery from his cradle. He had been toadied at Eton by boys whose fathers had sent them thither with that especial purpose; he had been sighed for (and had not denied them) by scores of young women of the middle class. The radicals, who pretend that an hereditary aristocracy is no better than any other section of the community, are in this the unconscious flatterers of the very class they would decry; for if those born with ' handles to their names' contrive, held aloft from the first by social sycophants, and exempt from the rubs of the world, to grow up to manhood as no *worse* than their fellow-creatures, that itself were a considerable feat, and would argue much in favour of the hereditary principle.

The Honourable Piers Mostyn had not been hitherto fortunate in making pecuniary profit out of his prefix; he had moved in somewhat too elevated circles; but he had a well-founded idea that he had only to show himself (with his card pinned to him) on the next *plateau* of society, to secure a wife with a suitable dower. At present, he had only received his share of ' that gigantic system of out-door relief for the aristocracy,' the Diplomatic Service, and the income thence derived had been wholly insufficient for his needs. These last were on a scale commensurate with his hereditary position.   His passion for gambling was intense, but he now had, unfortunately, not even a stake to risk; he had spent his patrimony of five thousand pounds in that pursuit, and already owed as much again for his necessary expenses. For the Honourable Piers Mostyn could not be maintained (nor did his country expect it) at the usual charges of an untitled gentleman; he was a fancy article, and was well aware, if the worst came to the worst, that he could fetch—in the matrimonial market—a fancy price.   In the mean time, he was madly in love.   Of course we do not use that term in the vulgar sense; it was not that sort of sentiment that takes up the harp of life, and 'smites the chord of self, which, trembling, fades in music out of sight.'   Far from it.   A more thoroughly selfish being than Piers Mostyn had become at two-and-twenty could scarcely be found, even among his own

frivolous and pampered class. Nor was his
passion of that sort which monopolizes its
possessor, to the exclusion of other female
objects of devotion. Among his eastern
friends in Persia, it was the custom to
marry a score or two of ladies, and yet
reserve one as the queen of the harem;
and our youthful diplomatist emulated
their example, as far as the more stolid
institutions of his native land permitted.
Gwendoline Treherne was his queen of the
harem, and he adored her above all the
rest. Her love for him was not only
grateful to him as a lover; it flattered his
vanity in a very high degree; for it was
quite on the cards that Gwendoline might
have been a duchess, had she directed her
marvellous energy and unrivalled charms to
the attainment of that end. A marriage
with her, even now, would have invested
him (for a fortnight or so) with considerable interest; the world (*his* world) would
have talked about it unceasingly, until

some other occurrence of an equally en-
thralling character turned up; but then,
unfortunately, one cannot live on *éclat*.

Marriage with Gwendoline had been
always impossible, but flirtation with her
had been by no means less pleasant upon
that account; quite the reverse; there had
been even a *soupçon* of impropriety about
it; it had been almost like making love to
somebody else's wife. And now that she
was absolutely engaged to be married, her
fascination for him was greatly increased.
The case of the man who adored pork, and
wished he was a Jew, in order that he
might have the additional pleasure of sin-
ning while he ate it, is not altogether an
exceptional one. When one has no other
pursuit than pleasure, innocent delights
soon begin to pall; when the appetite is
jaded, one takes to sauces *à la tartare*—to
sherry and bitters. Vice, of course, is
pleasant to everybody; but when it comes
to be pleasant because it *is* vice, matters

become serious, and require the attention
of the clergy. At present, however, the
Honourable Piers Mostyn had scarcely
reached this point, and we are perhaps doing his training an injustice in attributing
such a fruit to it so early. With all his
heart—with all the dregs of what he had
left in him in the way of sentiment—he
really did love Gwendoline Treherne. If
it had been possible for him to have made
any sacrifice whatever for the sake of
another person (which it was not), he
would have done it for her. He had not
seen her for a whole twelvemonth, and he
was now resolved to do so. He had suffered enough (he wrote) during that en-
forced estrangement, and he must hear the
music of her voice once more, and feel the
soft clasp of her hand. What possible
harm could there be in that, even in the
eyes of Mr Ferrier? He had been very
good and obedient to her hitherto; this one
interview was a very small reward for his

patient submission to her will, and he would have it.

Gwendoline was equally resolved that he should not have it. Her will was vastly stronger than his; but, on the other hand, his easy disposition would now and then, she knew, indulge itself in an outbreak of wilful obstinacy, with which it was very difficult to deal. Who has not experienced the sudden whims of a weak nature, and seen the ruin they have wrought in the plans of a stronger? And Gwendoline's plan was now threatened with such a catastrophe. She could not make Piers understand Mr Ferrier's nature—and indeed it had cost her months of assiduous study to learn it herself—nor dispossess him of the idea that his attentions to her would be considered by that respectable personage in the light of a compliment to himself. The old merchant was phlegmatic—not quick of observation, and conventional, as we have seen, in his views of society; but his respect for rank would never have induced him to forget his respect for himself. His ideas of right were fixed and absolute: he was not a man to be trifled with by anybody, and least of all, she felt, by a professional trifler like Piers Mostyn; for she was not less qualified to judge of Piers because his interests and her own were one. It was by no means unlikely, in short, that the latter's appearance at Bedivere Court might be the destruction of that social edifice of which she had with such infinite pains just laid the foundation, and she determined by all means to avoid an interview with him. At the same time, she could scarcely feel angry with her lover for conduct which, after all, was suggested by the love he professed, and which she herself reciprocated seven-fold.

'I forbid you to come to Cornwall,'

wrote she with earnest vehemence; 'and if you come, I will not see you.'

'I must come, however, and shall at all events see *you*,' was the infatuated young gentleman's reply.

CHAPTER XIV.

A PUBLIC CEREMONY.

It had not been Gwendoline's habit to mingle much with the society about Bedivere Court. She had not had many opportunities of doing so, for Sir Guy detested country amusements, and (so-called) gaieties, and of course she could not partake of them without his escort; moreover, there had been hitherto nothing to be got by them. But now that she was engaged to be married to a gentleman of the county, matters were very different. It was absolutely necessary that she should make herself popular in the neighbourhood of her future home, not merely for the sake of being well received as Mrs Ferrier of Glen Druid, but for ulterior reasons of a much more important kind. In the scheme of life that she had planned out for herself, the good opinion of the world, and especially that of her neighbours, must by all means be secured, and as large a fund of it laid up as possible; so that when the time came, she might be able to draw upon it for charitable excuses and a liberal construction of her own conduct. Sooner or later, she would have to present the cheques, and it was well to make arrangements as early as possible for getting them honoured. She never shut her eyes to the difficulties of her position, however far away they might lie, but did her very best from the first to smooth the way beforehand. It was pitiable indeed that so astute and prudent a general should be liable to disgrace and defeat, through the ignorant

impetuosity of such an ally as, Piers
Mostyn.

However, notwithstanding his rebellious
rejoinder to her last letter, she thought,
upon the whole, he would not venture to
force upon her that foolish 'just one' interview, which she felt might not alone be
dangerous in its consequences, but would
shake her own resolve to its foundation.
She was too proud and too wise to tell
him *that;* but the fact was she could not
trust herself to see him while it was yet
possible to become his wife. It was hard
enough to have to feign respectful affection
for Mr Ferrier, to have to receive with
smiles the congratulations of his friends, to
have to enter with apparent interest and
pleasure into plans for a future that she
looked upon with contemptuous aversion—
it was hard and bitter enough to have to
do all this in presence of the recollection
of the man she loved with such intensity
of passion; but to see him again face to

face, to speak with him, to press his hand, and perchance his lips, and *then* to turn away with a smothered sigh, and the full consciousness of the contrast, to become the wife of Mr Bruce Ferrier until death should them part, was an ordeal from which she shrank with shuddering. Had the case of herself and Piers been reversed, she would not perhaps have hesitated to place *him* in the same position; but then Gwendoline was a woman, and would have done so to triumph over her coming rival, whereas Piers Mostyn's design had only his own selfish wilfulness to excuse it.

Sir Guy and Miss Treherne, then, were now become much more sociable than their neighbours had hitherto found them to be, and the fact that they were so gave quite an impetus to the county hospitalities. Mr Ferrier was of course an invited guest on all these occasions, and it was more than once remarked what an earnest anxious glance his beautiful bride-elect would

throw round her as she entered such scenes
of gaiety, as if to see if her future lord
was there. The observers were correct
enough in their data, though not in their
conclusions. Gwendoline never joined a
pic-nic, nor an archery party, without casting one hurried, anxious gaze about her to
make sure that Piers Mostyn had not carried out his threat, and sought her presence
there. She had made up her mind what
to do even in such a case: she would have
taken his hand, and welcomed him as an
old friend, and as such introduced him to
Mr Ferrier. But could she rely upon herself to execute her own intentions? In
her secret heart, she did not think she
could; and hence it was that to keen spectators (such as happily 'the county' did
not afford) her face would seem to have
worn not only anxiety on such occasions,
but positive terror.

It was arranged that her marriage
should take place in London; and as the

autumn waned, the county gaieties, though of course they now mostly took an indoor shape, increased, until they became an almost unbroken round of farewell festivities, which it was well understood—without the least reflection on Cornish hospitality—would be returned with interest when the bride and bridegroom came to reside at home. There was still one outdoor *fête*, notwithstanding the inclement season, in connection with the great Glendallack copper-mines. The board of directors were mostly gentlemen of the county; and the completion of a tramway from the surface to nearly a mile under the sea had been the excuse for a great dinner and ball at the mansion of one of the largest shareholders. The ceremony itself was not without local interest, and attracted a vast number of spectators from St Medards and other places, for hitherto the mine had been worked only by the usual method of levels and ladders; and the introduction of a

wheeled carriage into its subterranean
depths was an event in its history. It was
understood that some of the ladies of the
neighbourhood, including Miss Trehorne,
would condescend to use this novel con-
veyance; but when they came to look at
the vehicle in question, and the road which
it had to travel, the determination of most
of them gave way. Imagine a tramway
descending across the face of a bleak cliff
at an angle of forty-five degrees; for a
hundred yards or so, the sheer crag was on
one side, and on the other—with no sort
of wall or guard—the winter sea ; beyond
that was what looked like a small black
hole, through which the vehicle disappeared
to finish the rest of its journey in pitch
darkness beneath the cliff and the ocean. A
princess as courageous as charming, has
achieved the adventure of late years, but
at that time no member of the female sex
had ever visited the dark depths of Glendallack; nor was it to be wondered at that

they shrank upon this occasion from the steep unprotected way and the black portal.

The car, as it was euphuistically called, was by no means an attractive equipage. It was a small carriage, or rather truck, of solid iron, which would hold with comfort —if such a term be not totally out of place —six persons, two and two, sitting very close behind each other. It was let down and pulled up by means of a stationary engine working an endless chain. Most of the fair visitors had of course expected to find a first-class saloon railway carriage, and a level road agreeably lighted up for their convenience; and it did not tend to promote their confidence when they were informed that the car fitted almost as closely into the tunnel before them as a bullet in a gun, so that they must not move hand or foot while passing through it. Lastly, it was necessary to put over their fine clothes certain garments, very considerate-

ly made for the occasion, but still neither
elegant nor becoming. As for the gentlemen, they were provided with regular
miners' attire. Under the circumstances,
out of the dozen fine ladies who had come
to Glendallack with the expressed intention of going down in the car, and who
saw the preparations made for their descent
in presence of an admiring throng, ten
unhesitatingly declined to make the venture. They were very sorry, they said, to
disappoint the public, but the public would
survive it, whereas they felt confident they
themselves never should. When pressed,
they took a still more dignified attitude,
and refused upon the ground of religious
principle. It was all very well for persons whose business lay in such places
to go down there twice a day after tin
and copper (or 'whatever it was'), but
in their own case they felt it would be
'tempting Providence.' In vain it was
urged that it was a wrong view to take of

that beneficent power to suppose that it is always ready to do us an ill turn when it catches us at a disadvantage ; they had no wish to argue the matter, they replied, but they would stay above-ground, and out of harm's way.

Gwendoline alone, and Miss Blackett, expressed their intention of carrying out the programme; an announcement that was received with enthusiasm by the public at large, and with solemn head-shakes and doleful warnings by their recusant sisters. It was a most dangerous and foolhardy adventure ; and if Mr Ferrier had been there (which on this particular occasion he did not happen to be, but was closeted with his lawyer at Glen Druid), they were sure he would never have permitted Miss Treherne to undertake it. As for Miss Blackett, ' she was old enough to know better ; ' or indeed, some did not hesitate to whisper that the idea of getting a beau all to herself, on whom she could lean and confide

throughout the journey, was so attractive a
bait to that excellent but somewhat ancient
maiden lady, that it had overcome her
fears. We do not venture to say whether
this was or was not the reason. She
averred that she went solely to take care
of her brother, who was infatuated with
Miss Treherne, and had foolishly consti-
tuted himself her escort. But in the case
of Gwendoline, the possible danger of the
trip was itself the chief attraction : she
welcomed any excitement, because it prevented her from dwelling upon her own
thoughts, and the more strange and stir-
ing it was, the better it pleased her.

It was amid great cheering that the two
ladies, having retired into the manager's
house to put on their dress, reappeared
upon the platform *en costume*, and were
presently followed by the similarly meta-
morphosed gentlemen. With respect to
Gwendoline, whatever she put on anew
seemed to become her best. She looked

as though that tight-fitting flannel gown
and solid wide-awake had been donned expressly to enhance her charms, and a buzz
of involuntary admiration greeted her as
she stepped with a quiet smile whither
the car was standing ready for departure.
If her companion's personal appearance
had not similarly improved, it, at all events,
had not suffered much damage. But that
of the male adventurers was sorely deterior-
ated. The expression 'Nature's gentlemen' had probably no reference to costume;
otherwise, we must deny its application,
even to the most noble-looking of mortals,
when rigged out in a suit of coarse white
sailcloth, and surmounted by a solid round
hat with a tallow-candle stuck in the brim.

The company who were to make the
first trip consisted of six persons, arranged
in the following order : in the first seat,
Miss Blackett and a Mr Kerr of St Medards were to place themselves ; in the
second, Miss Treherne and Mr Blackett ;

and behind were the brakesman and a guide for the underground passages. There was no room for any one else; but the narrow stone steps that ran by the side of the tramway into the mine, and which had hitherto formed the only mode of ingress and egress, were crowded all along, down to the very mouth of the tunnel, with workmen. Poor Mr Blackett, who, compared with his energetic sister, might have been almost said to be the less masculine of the two, nervous, dyspeptic, and quite unaccustomed to publicity, exhibited at this supreme moment, just as the car was about to move, a truly pitiable spectacle. He was devoted, in his feeble sentimental way, to Gwendoline (who was aware of his existence, and that was all), and in an evil moment of chivalrous enthusiasm, he had volunteered to be her escort down Glendallack; but he now bitterly repented himself of that hazardous undertaking. He shuddered, not so much from the nipping and eager air which the wintry sunshine could not warm, as with the terrors of the prospect before him. The steepness of the incline; the roaring and dashing of the sea immediately beneath him, and into which it seemed as likely they would slide off as not; the small black hole into which they had presently to enter, and that looked scarcely large enough to accommodate the car even without its inmates; and the unimaginable terrors of the mine itself, appalled him. As he sat staring blankly before him, with two tallow-candles stuck in his hard round hat, he looked like some badly executed patron saint in wax, to whom a poor but pious neighbourhood had devoted their dips without conciliating him. At the very last moment, he suddenly jumped up, and made an effort to get out of the car. He had already adjured Gwendoline not to persist in going down the mine, and protested, with all the eloquence which truth inspires, that for her sake he would give up the adventure without a pang of regret; and she had quietly announced her intention of going through with it. He had washed his hands, therefore, of all responsibility— so far as she was concerned—and had nothing to consult but his own precious personal safety. A roar of disapprobation arose when his intention was discovered: there was a moment of indecision, in which he seemed to Gwendoline (who mercifully averted her eyes) to get out and get in again, and the machine began to move slowly down the incline.

It really was a nervous moment: to the tenants of the car it seemed as if they were gliding into the sea itself; and Miss Blackett clung to Mr Kerr, as though he were *her* patron saint, and should be propitiated whether he would or not. But, after the first moment, Gwendoline began to enjoy it; the roaring wind, the leaping spray, the black rock in front, that seemed

to yawn for those that were about to ex-
plore its secrets, seemed to string her
nerves and stir her blood. For the first
time in all her life she recognized what it
was to be face to face with the great powers
of nature; vigorous of mind and strong of
will though she was, her whole existence
had hitherto been artificial; her intellect
had never been braced by one broad
thought; she had been hemmed in by con-
vention from her cradle, and no yearning
to escape from its dull round had ever
visited her. What all her life had been,
now suddenly contrasted itself in her
mind with another sort of life, of which
she had only read. How would it be with
her now, had she always passed her days
with honest simple folk, who lived mostly
in the open air amid such sights and sounds
as were now about her?

> O well for the sailor lad
> That he sings in his boat on the bay!

some poet had written, and those words

came back to her with a far other and deeper meaning than they had ever had before. 'Would it not have been well for *her* if, instead of the life she was now living—outwardly so gay and pleasant, but inwardly one net of fraud and lies—a life in whose atmosphere she never seemed to draw one natural breath—' The car had already glided under the little tunnel, into warmth indeed, but total gloom, a type of the very existence which she was picturing; but ere she could continue her reflections, a hand was lightly laid on hers, and a voice which she well knew, and which thrilled every fibre of her frame with anger, and joy, and fear, whispered : 'Gwendoline!'

CHAPTER XV.

DOWN GLENDALLACK.

AT the same moment wherein Gwendoline became conscious that Piers Mostyn, and not Mr Blackett, was sitting beside her in the car, the machine was suddenly brought to a full stop, for the purpose of lighting the candles which, in the open air, would at once have been extinguished. Even when all were provided with these beacons, they did little more than make the rugged roof immediately above them visible, and cast a feeble glimmer upon the wet walls. When Miss Blackett turned round to ejaculate: 'Horrible; is it not,

Alec?' she would not, perhaps, have discovered that Alexander had decided upon
limiting his conquests to the earth's surface, and had left the guardianship of her
friend to another; Piers, not knowing
what line to take, remained silent, but
Gwendoline replied promptly for him:
' Your brother is not here; he was afraid
of catching cold, I suppose.'

' Oh, I see; one of the workmen has
taken his place. Well, perhaps it's better
so, my dear. You will be in safer hands,
for Alec is quite unfitted for these sort of
expeditions: I told him so when he proposed it.—O my goodness! Mr Kerr'
(and she gave her neighbour a most
genuine squeeze), ' if we ain't going lower
still!'

Considering that they had only just
entered the mine, this was not to be wondered at; but the fact was, as poor Miss
Blackett subsequently observed, ' she had
seemed to have passed a lifetime in the

dreadful place already,' and could do nothing throughout the journey but pinch
Mr Kerr, and say her prayers. Her attention and that of her companion being
thus entirely absorbed, Piers and Gwendoline were left to converse almost as freely
as if they had been alone, except for the
brakesman and his assistant, who had
other matters to engage their minds.

'How dare you come here, Piers?'

'Because I love you, dearest. Orpheus
went down to a similar locality—to see his
wife; and I have come here to see *you*. I
really could not resist it, my own darling.'

Gwendoline did not withdraw her hand
from his warm pressure—she could not
deny herself so great a pleasure; but her
tone had much resentment in it still, as
she replied: 'It was a most dangerous and
foolish thing to do, Piers. Does any one
know of your being here?'

'Not a soul save the brakesman behind
us, and he does not know who I am. I

said I wished to go down the mine, and they gave me this dress, and bade me wait for the next car. If "Alec" (who's Alec?) had not got out, I should have come down the ladder, and taken my chance of seeing you. How beautiful you look with that star upon your forehead, like a goddess.'

'Do I? I cannot return the compliment: Miss Blackett took you for one of the workmen.'

'Bless her. So will everybody else, I hope. I wish I *was* a workman; that is, if you were also employed on the same level. I could travel to the centre of the earth like this, and enjoy it beyond everything.'

'Could you?' Gwendoline was pouting; but he missed that from the insufficient supply of light. 'Then you cannot be much devoted to scenery.'

'I see your face, darling, and that is the fairest scene to be beheld upon earth— or beneath it. Confound it! we are stop-

ping again. These people will insist upon
our going to look at something.'

Never was explorer of mine so easily
satisfied as Piers Mostyn. He would have
been content to have been lowered through
scores of miles of mere tunnel, and then
dragged up again. He wished to see nothing but the face beside him—to hear
nothing but that voice, which was certainly growing less resentful, and even
almost tender towards him. But Science
is a severe schoolmistress, who has no
patience with such ridiculous follies, and
must be listened to whenever she speaks.
The brakesman's assistant had had his
orders to 'explain Glendallack' to the
distinguished visitors of the day, and he
conscientiously did it. It was like hearing
a lecture at the Polytechnic. But never
had those instructive walls contained so
unheedful an audience. Miss Blackett
was otherwise engaged, as we know, and
could not listen. Mr Kerr had shares in

the mine, and knew all about it. Gwendoline was staring straight before her, looking (if there had been light enough to see) haggard rather than bored: she almost wished that the rope would break, and the enigma of her life be solved in that fashion. Piers, beneath his silken moustache, was muttering curses in the Parisian tongue. The brakesman's assistant having premised that he was unaccustomed to speak in public, discoursed with a fluency that could only have been acquired by constant practice. He had himself a smattering of science, and had invented something—a pump, or a valve, or a coupling-chain—of which he had a model at home, and would be happy to show it to the ladies and gentlemen when they got above-ground.

'Ah, if ever we *do*,' sighed Miss Blackett. She was a thrifty soul, but she would have given ten golden guineas at that moment to have been in a position to

behold the model referred to. Happy
Alec! He was a coward, but not a fool;
he was on *terra firma*, and not under it.
How she hated Mr Kerr, who must have
known where he was bringing her to!
Heaven might forgive him, but she certainly did not make that special request
in his favour. Why was it so frightfully
hot, and ;what was that which was drop-
ping on her head and shoulders from the
roof? She interrupted the torrent of the
lecturer's eloquence, to ask these two
questions.

'Well, mum, as for the heat, that is
said to arise from our propinquity to a
very hot place indeed.'

'Great Heaven deliver us!' exclaimed
Miss Blackett fervently.

'No, mum; it is not the place you are
thinking on : I was referring to the Central
Fire. The warm air we are breathing,
however, although inconvenient to parties
unaccustomed to it, is not hurtful. As for

the iron drippings, they are quite harmless.'

'But what do they *come* from, man?' urged the poor lady.

'Well, they come from the sea, mum: we are half a mile out or more under the waves. The faint hollow boom you would hear—if you were to listen very quiet—is the noise of the sea above your head.'

'Just so, my man,' said Mr Kerr with the patronizing tone of a proprietor. 'Now, will you tell us how many feet of rock, in the roof here, lie between us and the water?'

'Well, where you are pointing, sir, about six feet; but where that wooden plug is put, *not above three*. If I was to knock it away this moment—'

An agonized cry broke forth from Mr Kerr. 'My *dear* Miss Blackett, you ran a pin into me!'

'I know I did,' exclaimed that lady with the calmness of despair; 'and I'll do it again, if you don't make that man leave off, and instantly take us up again. You ought to be ashamed of yourself for bringing ladies into such a place at all. The idea of one's trusting to a wooden plug! I am sure I have turned quite gray within the last five minutes.'

If Mr Kerr had had any action at law brought against him by the lady, on the ground of this personal damage to her charms, it is possible he might have produced witnesses to prove that she was turning gray some time previous to her descent into Glendallack; but he was much too gallant as well as prudent to hint at anything of the sort just now.

'My dear madam,' answered he, 'I assure you there is not the slightest danger. People are working all along yonder gallery, and do so every day, just as safely as though they were digging potatoes in their own gardens: nobody gets so far as this down the mine without leaving the .

carriage and going to see them. We must take back with us some memento of our visit, in the shape of a bit of tin or copper ore. Come—let me give you my arm— and see the specimens hammered out with our own eyes.'

'I don't move one step out of this car for all the wealth of Golconda; and you don't either, Mr Kerr,' added Miss Blackett hastily: 'I am not going to be left alone in this place for a single instant.—What do *you* say, Miss Treherne? You have had enough of these dreadful proceedings, I am sure: no young woman with any sense of propriety would wish for any more; with the candles all guttering down as they are, and not likely to last a bit longer than we want them to do.'

'I am quite at your service, Miss Blackett,' said Gwendoline quietly. 'It is a matter of perfect indifference to me whether we remain or return.'

'Then let us go back at once, man,' exclaimed Miss Blackett.

'Just as you please, mum,' returned the brakesman's assistant. 'Only, if you won't go to the workings, you will never be sure that the specimen you buy above-ground was really found here. But I'll just knock you down a lump or two from the roof—'

Again a cry of irrepressible agony broke forth from the unhappy Mr Kerr. 'This confounded woman—that is, I mean this lady here,' said he, correcting himself, 'is exceedingly timid, my man. Give the signal to draw up at once—*immediately*—do you hear me?'

'I am sorry if I have hurt you,' said Miss Blackett, reserving her apology until the machine began sensibly to ascend; 'but I really couldn't help it: I would have done the same if it had been the lord-lieutenant.'

' I wish it *had* been the lord-lieutenant, madam, with all my heart,' returned Mr Kerr viciously, and continuing to rub his leg, for the pin had, this time, hurt him exceedingly.

Nature is often complimented upon making so many folks, and yet none of them (save her twins) altogether similar in feature; but the variety of character with which she dowers us is infinitely greater. Even twins are sometimes of totally opposite dispositions.

The little car that was now toiling up from the depths of Glendallack was bringing what auctioneers call 'a very mixed lot' to join their fellows above-ground. That Mr Kerr was of the same flesh and blood as his companion, she indeed had proved to his great inconvenience; but beyond that they had scarcely anything in common. He was a gambler in railway and mining shares, and speculative even in his religious opinions. She was prudent and orthodox, but devoted to sixpenny loo, from which he shrank, as being an immoral dissipation. The brakesman, again, who had been specially imported from a distance, on account of his great gifts in his particular line, was almost as much a machine as the invention he controlled and admired as the perfection of human skill; while his companion and assistant was a Brunel in embryo, dissatisfied with every mechanical institution as ineffectual, and only not guilty of ruining railway companies with his ingenious novelties, because the opportunity had not as yet been afforded him.

> The applause of board-room meetings to command,
>   The threats of loss and ruin to despise,

his lot forbade; but he yearned to wade through treasure to the throne of chief-engineer, and to shut the gates of Economy on the British shareholder.

Like the ham of the sandwich, Piers and Gwendoline, between these two differing pairs, most certainly partook of the qualities of neither; nor, perhaps, though they had a common interest in life, which the others lacked, were their characters, on the whole, more similar.

'I am glad to have seen you, and pressed your hand, dear Gwendoline, at all events,' murmured Piers. 'This must last me for some time, I suppose.'

Passionately as Gwendoline loved this man, it was perhaps a part of her punishment for doing so that her keen eyes were not closed to his faults—that is, to those shortcomings, which, measured even by the moral standard which *she* used, were faults. She well knew that he was inordinately selfish; but that phrase of his, 'last me,' just as she was about to part from him on the cross-road of life, sent a chill to her very heart. Her silence, and the sudden relaxing of the fingers which lay in his grasp, at once informed him of his error.

'Dearest Gwendoline,' continued he

tenderly, 'do not think me selfish, for you and I—as it seems to me—are one. When far away from you, I have only the recollection of you to comfort me : I seem but half myself, and that the worse half. When —when may I hope to see you again?'

'I do not know, Piers; perhaps never. I wish that I could die this moment—thus, with my hand in yours.' She was dreadfully agitated : she was trembling in every limb for the love and the loss of him ; and he knew it.

'No, no, dearest; you shall live on. We will be happy together yet: do not doubt it. When—when are you coming to town?'

'Papa and I go the beginning of next month. Mr Ferrier follows us, with the children. The marriage is to take place on the 20th.'

'And I am not to see you betwixt this and then?'

'Certainly not, Piers. If you have one

single spark of genuine love for me, you
will avoid me, not only betwixt now and
then, but for months to come. We shall
be in Italy for a long time. I will write
to you; but you must not write to me. It
is a small thing enough to ask of you,
Piers, in return for much; but will you
promise me *that?*'

'I will, dear; I do. But you will
think of me; you will not forget me,
Gwendoline?'

'Forget you? No, Piers.—Ah me!'
(she muttered to herself) ' would to Heaven
I could!'

'You are shivering, dearest: I trust
this confounded place has not given you
cold. I feel the draught myself: we must
be getting near the day-light. I do not
say good-bye, darling—*au revoir.*'

Their hands parted with a tender
squeeze, and not a moment too soon. The
candles began to pale, the gloom to thin,
the fresh salt air to make itself felt. Amid

the sound of beating waves, and blowing winds, and cheering human voices, the car was drawn up to the platform whence it had started. An immense crowd welcomed their arrival; among whom, though modestly keeping in the second rank, were Mr and Mrs Samuel Barland, the latter of whom always made a point of patronizing all entertainments that were gratuitous.

'You are looking rather white, Miss Treherne,' said Mr Kerr, as he assisted her to alight. 'I trust you were not as frightened as Miss Blackett; though, if you were, I am sure you behaved yourself better.—Hollo! what has become of your friend?—Brakesman, here is something for yourself, and for your assistant also; and, although as it happened there was nothing for him to do, here is a couple of shillings for the other workman. He has mixed with the rest, and I can't tell one man from the other; but you will see he gets it.'

None present had the slightest suspicion

that Gwendoline had gone down Glendallack with Piers Mostyn sitting by her side.
Mrs Barland, however, did remark, as her
husband and herself trudged home together
that afternoon: ' Yon was a bonnie laddie
that took Mr Blackett's place by Miss Treherne, eh? Did you ever see him before?'

' I dare say,' was Mr Barland's careless
reply. ' There's a matter of six hundred
men as works at Glendallack, and most of
'em comes to our shop when their insides
wants looking to. You're a nice young
woman, *you* are, to be so curious about
" bonnie laddies," and only a six-months'
bride yourself! I am downright ashamed
of you, Susan.' But he did not look
ashamed of her by any means, but regarded
her, head aside, with complacent criticism,
as an investment with which he had every
reason to be satisfied.

' Nay, it wasn't so much his bonnie
face that took me, Sam. But I thought it
unco strange that he should have flitted

away without staying to get his siller from Mr Kerr.'

Mr Samuel Barland's philosophic face relaxed into a smile, and his gray eyes twinkled with merriment, as he tapped the ashes out of his pipe, and observed approvingly: 'It's plain ye come from the far north, Susan.'

END OF VOL. I.

JOHN CHILDS AND SON, PRINTERS.